PENGUIN BOOKS

OBLIVION

Josephine Hart was born and educated in Ireland.
In the 1960s she worked in publishing in London,
becoming a director of Haymarket Publishing. She
has also produced several successful West End
plays, including the award-winning *The House of
Bernarda Alba* and Iris Murdoch's *The Black Prince*,
and many poetry productions, as well as hosting
Thames TV's *Books By My Bedside*. She is the author
of two internationally bestselling novels, *Damage*,
which was made into a major movie, and *Sin*.
Josephine Hart is married to Maurice Saatchi and
has two sons. She lives in London and Sussex.

JOSEPHINE HART

OBLIVION

PENGUIN BOOKS

PENGUIN BOOKS

Published by the Penguin Group

Penguin Books USA Inc., 375 Hudson Street, New York, New York 10014, U.S.A.
Penguin Books Ltd, 27 Wrights Lane, London W8 5TZ, England
Penguin Books Australia Ltd, Ringwood, Victoria, Australia
Penguin Books Canada Ltd, 10 Alcorn Avenue, Toronto, Ontario, Canada M4V 3B2
Penguin Books (N.Z.) Ltd, 182–190 Wairau Road, Auckland 10, New Zealand

Penguin Books Ltd, Registered Offices: Harmondsworth, Middlesex, England

First published in Great Britain by Chatto & Windus Limited 1995
First published in the United States of America by Viking Penguin,
a division of Penguin Books USA Inc. 1995
Published in Penguin Books 1997

3 5 7 9 10 8 6 4 2

PUBLISHER'S NOTE
This is a work of fiction. Names, characters, places, and incidents either are the
product of the author's imagination or are used fictitiously, and any resemblance to
actual persons, living or dead, events, or locales is entirely coincidental.

Grateful acknowledgment is made for permission to reprint
excerpts from the following copyrighted works:
"After Laura" from Selections from "The Canzioniere" and Other Works by Petrarch,
translated by Mark Musa. By permission of Oxford University Press. "No Time" from
W. H. Auden: Collected Poems. Copyright © 1941 by W. H. Auden. Reprinted by
permission of Random House, Inc. "Buffalo Bill's" from Complete Poems 1904–1962 by
E. E. Cummings, edited by George J. Firmage. Copyright © 1976, 1991 by the
Trustees for the E. E. Cummings Trust and George James Firmage. Reprinted by
permission of W. W. Norton & Company Ltd. "After You've Gone," words and music
by Turner Layton and Henry Creamer, Morley Music Co. "The Pity of Love" and "The
Spur" from The Poems of W. B. Yeats: A New Edition edited by Richard J. Finneran.
Copyright 1940 by Georgie Yeats, renewed 1968 by Bertha Georgie Yeats, Michael
Butler Yeats, and Anne Yeats. Reprinted with permission of Scribner, a division of
Simon & Schuster Inc. "In Plaster" from Crossing the Water by Sylvia Plath. Copyright ©
1971 by Ted Hughes. Reprinted by permission of HarperCollins Publishers, Inc. and
Faber & Faber Ltd. "Aubade" and "An Arundel Tomb" by Philip Larkin from Collected
Poems, published by Farrar, Straus & Giroux, Inc. and Faber & Faber Ltd.

Printed in the United States of America
Set in Perpetua

FOR M.

AS ALWAYS

ONE

This is an elegant room. Is this is an elegant room? Absorb the colour blue. Mark the dark blue curtains, light blue bedspread, the fine chairs, upholstered in pale grey silk.

Now, listen for sound. Note the rain on the tiny balcony. As though orchestrated, it beats a rhythm on the tiles. Listen to the music.

What am I doing here? Oh, God, why did I think I could do this? I must do this. Others have done this. It is a rite of passage.

Concentrate. I am here because of my desire. Say it to yourself. I am here because of my desire.

Now, concentrate on your nakedness. I am . . . am I here? Desire is here, but am I here? I have been shattered, as though I were a pane of glass to which someone had taken a hammer. Could desire reassemble me? Does the body, just the body, have a soul? I'm looking for the smallest truth, then I can, perhaps, move on.

My desire to be here is genuine. I have genuine desire: this at least is true. After all, the body does not lie in these matters. And in these matters, a man's body is a more truthful map than a woman's. My body is more truthful than hers. But I believe she desires me too. There is little proof at this stage. At this moment I stand opposite her in a hotel bedroom. I am naked, therefore my desire is known. She is naked, but her desire is hidden. The desire of women is always hidden. Except in her eyes?

Where will I lead her? Where in this room shall we lie down together? On the floor, or on the bed, on its pale blue cover? Or will desire overcome us and shall we lie against the wall? Can I do this? I do not know. And there will be discoveries before such a decision is possible, discoveries which will determine the outcome. Physical discoveries of the strength, the pliability, the suppleness and speed of the body opposite mine. When I have made these discoveries, they will move us finally towards the vertical or horizontal, hard or soft meeting place, of this particular two, made one.

I move a number of steps closer to her and stop. She does not take a step back. And my desire mixes for a moment with gratitude for her grace and it is a sweet feeling. I have not known sweetness since beyond a point in my memory which I do not visit. I look at her body. I try to see her body. I try to clear the haze that sometimes clouds the eye when desire, now almost blind, panics for the sense of touch. I resist. I continue to look and to see. I concentrate on the sight of her. She is tall. We are virtually the same height. I must concentrate only on her. Her shoulders are thin and they slope slightly. Her breasts are small and pointed. I concentrate on them. I move closer. I bow my head and suck her right nipple. She does not move away. She raises herself a little on her toes. To help me, I believe. And the sweetness comes again and settles itself into my desire, an undernote of a most unexpected nature.

I move my mouth to her left nipple and now caress her right breast with the fingers of my left hand. I concentrate totally on these actions and on the sensations they elicit. Now I listen to certain sounds she is making. A chorus of the breath. Short then slow, then fast then nothing, then a panting that flutters somewhere in her throat and which I can almost hear, as she bends her neck and head towards mine. Taste and touch and sound mingle in my mind. And concentration has taken me to this point. And, at this point, I know only her.

I move to kneel before her. I press my face into her stomach. It is as pale and flat as the white of a page. It is the stomach of youth and nothing has been written on it. I move my head down and past the hip bones and I move my mouth onto and into the hair, then my tongue onto and into her. I know now that she feels desire and that in a sense the first step to oneness has been taken. My tongue unites me with her. I listen to the sounds above me. And I stop. I remember what they are telling me. I remember what my tongue knows from the swelling it encounters now. I remember. And, now, I do not know only her.

You are here. You are here with us. And I am trapped here with her. You cannot stay here. It is not right. You cannot stay here with me. I desired you, I always desired you. I desired you in the body of your long-legged teenage triumph and in the body of your formal power of wife. I was unusual, I desired my wife. Oh my darling, now I see you in your body fertile, filled up, bursting. And I can see again your aggressive stomach, that swelled but only for a short time. Was that loss a harbinger of the other, more terrible loss? Now your later body is here, too, and I want to weep for it. I am nailed weeping, perhaps forever, to that grey vision of your body battling, formidable, then lessening, ever lessening, on and on to less and less. And then, your body quiet: the quietest quiet I will ever know. Where did all the swelling go to? And all that rising and falling? Where did it all go to? How did it come to such an end? Come to me. Come back to me. Oh, please, come back and stay with me. Come to me. Come to me.

Oh, God, I'm tired. I lay the girl on the floor. I don't have the strength to move her to another place. More truthfully, I no longer have the inclination. I'm tired. I am so tired. I lie above her as though to hide her from you, darling. I do not want to hurt you. And as I slide into her, the ruthlessness sickens me and yet I cannot stop. She moves a little, in her generosity, to accommodate me. I know that she is close to what I would most willingly bring her. You are angry. You turn to leave. Come back, come back, forgive me. Please forgive me. Please come back to me. Come back. Come. Come.

And she came. And you didn't. And you never will.

TWO

The girl's name is Sarah. I like her name, but I cannot use it in certain situations. It is a substantial name, a name that implies a certain reliability. Though a fashionable name for daughters, its biblical connotations still survive.

I have now met her father, George Bonnington. He is wary of me. He is right. 'I mean no harm. I have no wish to harm her.' I'd like to say that to him. Man to man, as they say. But I think he knows 'Most things are never meant', and he knows that consequences are mostly unforeseen, and that to wish to do no harm is not the same as not doing any. And most certainly not the same as doing good.

I like George Bonnington very much, and I respect him. I respect his work. He is a surgeon. He takes away from the body to recreate a seared face; or to disguise the cancer cicatrice. George Bonnington is a sculptor of the human body and he uses a scalpel to do his work. Yet he makes no comment on those who wish to use his skills for the improvement of their perfectly adequate faces. They are too easy to condemn. They simply long for a dream of themselves. He says yes and helps them. But for one day a week only.

I like him for that. It shows the sweetness that I see in his daughter, a desire to help even those unworthy of it. I admire his determined athleticism in late middle-age. "Would you like to undergo six hours in theatre with an unfit surgeon? It's ninety per cent stamina and ten per cent skill," he lies. I admire his elegance, "A compliment to my patients." He is a man who knows beyond all doubt that life is worth living and worth fighting for.

Sarah's mother's name is Grace. Grace has the pastel-prettiness of a certain kind of Englishwoman – the hues so understated that only over time does one become conscious of their perfection. Grace works as a counsellor to couples in trouble. As one who has had a long and happy marriage, she is perhaps a symbol of its possibility in a world of unbelievers. Whether she can understand their agony I do not know, but I'm told she is effective in her work.

Grace is always kind to me during my rare visits to their house in Richmond. Her kindness arises out of her sense of justice – I am innocent until proven guilty and, as yet, there has been no crime.

Grace and George Bonnington – the good parents of a good daughter, Sarah. She and they are to be treasured. I break no laws in being at the outer edges of their lives and less deeply into Sarah's than she would wish, neither the laws of state nor those of God, as I understand them.

My work is not much respected and certainly not as much as George Bonnington's. Though I am well rewarded financially, I suppose my work is only enviable in that it has brought me a modicum of fame. Fame is a tiny pleasure, 'A mathematical equation whereby you are known by more people than you know', but a pleasure none the less.

I am, I believe, well established as a feature writer on a major newspaper. Some years ago, I was invited to present a series of profiles for radio called *Directions*, a programme which examined key moments in the lives of prominent men and women – in politics, the arts, the professions – which forced them to change direction. The programme became a considerable success. The effect of my occasionally over-incisive questions was tempered by my supposedly appealing voice, and the audience followed my promotion to television. I found its light not quite so blinding as I had previously imagined. I stepped centre stage, or more accurately to the position marked out for me by an irate production manager who believed I was dry as dust. I spoke my first words to all those I would never know, but who would now believe they knew me. A subsequent, late-night programme called *After Words* further established my reputation as a reliable, though occasionally, provocative presenter. *Directions* and *After Words* did well and I became a 'star', 'when only one is shining in the sky', as you used to tease me. And you used to tease me a lot . . .

THREE

Sarah does not tease me. Or perhaps, more truthfully, I will not let her. There are a number of things which I will not let Sarah do. I do not let her link her fingers through mine, though I will and often do hold her hand. I will not visit France with her, though we have been to Rome. When I sleep with her, which is never in my home, there is a certain way of lying together which I cannot allow.

Sarah believes that time and patience will change these things. Because she is young, she believes that time is her ally. And though she is young, she believes she can learn patience. For Sarah has the habit of youth, the habit of hope. She has, you might say, a bias towards the future.

It is not fair for a young woman to be forced to learn the only lesson I now seem able to teach. When I tell her this, she smiles — that marvellous smile of those who understand, but who are without experience; who know

what the words say but who have missed the meaning.
And when she gleans from my face or my physical
reaction that all is not well, she whispers the words
which, never innocent, always demand a response: "I
love you, I truly love you." "I know." An arrogant and
selfish reply, but what would you have me say? "I love
you too." Though of course, in a way, I do. Daily, I
come to believe a little more in her belief that I may love
her. She seems to have such certainty. Sarah believes in
love. She believes in its power. As I do. Sometimes, I
resent her almost clever unselfishness, her calm accept-
ance of my sudden departures from her pretty, carefully
organized little flat in Kensington – even after having
made love. At other times, I am grateful, selfishly
grateful.

It is, as they say, early days. As though the beginning
ever determined the end. As though time has an intimate
and benign part to play in the individual life, now that we
no longer believe in an individual God. So, I listen to
Sarah and I look at her and I concentrate.

Evidently, my life 'must go on'. I've said it to others
in the past and I hear it now. It sounds different.

FOUR

I always loved your name, Laura. Oh, how I loved your name. My first gift to you, when I had a little money, was a silver-framed, fourteenth-century poem that celebrated your name. It still sits beside my bed, in the same position on the table, just slightly to the left of the clock you gave me. Tick tock.

> When I summon my sighs to call for you,
> with that name Love inscribed upon my heart,
> in 'LAudable' the sound at the beginning
> of the sweet accents of that word come forth.
>
> Your 'REgal' state which I encounter next
> doubles my strength for the high enterprise;
> but 'TAcitly' the end cries, 'for her honour
> needs better shoulders for support than yours.'
>
> And so, to 'LAud' and to 'REvere' the word

itself instructs whenever someone calls you,
O lady worthy of all praise and honour,
unless, perhaps, Apollo be incensed
that 'morTAl' tongue be so presumptuous
to speak of his eternally green boughs.

Years later I thought it a terrible omen that I came across another poem from Petrarch's *Canzoniere* — 'After Laura's Death'. I always loved your name, Laura. Oh Laura, Laura, how I loved to say your name. "My wife's name is Laura." "I'd like you to meet my wife, Laura." "Hello, I'm Laura," you'd say. And hold your hand out and beam at people. You had a shocking smile, Laura. Sometimes you looked so happy it was shocking. And sometimes, Laura, in your frozen anger over something, anything, you were shockingly cold and arrogant. Oh, Laura, Laura. Now, I suppose I'd have to say, "My wife's name was Laura." "Was?" "Yes, she's dead." "Oh, dear, I am sorry — I'm truly sorry." "Thank you." "Were you married long?" "We were married for just over twelve years." "Any children?" "No," after a pause, again, "No. She was only twenty when we married. She was a physiotherapist . . . In a practice in Wimpole Street . . . She was clever and kind . . . She looked wonderful in her white coat . . . She . . .

We . . ." And I'd stop there. It is enough. For I know if I asked them in half an hour "What was my wife's name?" they'd have forgotten. Why should they remember? But I forget nothing. I will forget nothing. Laura Bolton, née Rowden, you have been dead for just over a year. Daughter of Jane and Jack Rowden, who became my parents-in-law. What is their titular position now? Are they still my parents-in-law? So many ripples in the lake. Will your mother now be less circumspect in her behaviour towards me? Will she still show her slight contempt? Was it contempt?

FIVE

"Andrew."

"Yes."

"It's Jack. Have you got a moment?"

"Yes, of course."

"I wonder if we could meet for a drink. There's something I'd like to discuss with you."

"Yes. Yes, of course." Does the speed of my response hide the slight reluctance in my voice?

"My club. Tomorrow? Sixish?"

"Fine."

There was a time when I blushed to meet Jack Rowden in the street, burning with some shame I never felt when I was with his daughter, Laura, when I did the things I knew he guessed I did with his daughter, Laura.

He never liked me. A man with a First in Greats who becomes a trusted servant of the Crown will bring a certain disdain to his conversations with a man who has a

2.2 in English from Bristol and who works in 'The Media'. Or is that unworthy thought just another example of the slight feeling of inferiority he has always engendered in me? Perhaps I have known him for too long. Perhaps for too long I was the other man in his daughter's life. A position we both thought I would keep forever.

In the hours after your shockingly short battle ended, Laura, when I wept and said, "We've both lost her," never was the difference between us as men, more profound. He is, perhaps, a Greek. I am a Roman.

You always knew he was a philanderer, Laura. I was more appalled than you were by his behaviour. And stunned by the almost insolent way he once acknowledged me in a restaurant, when he was accompanied by one of his women. We've kept our distance through all these years. I was not his ideal son-in-law. In his eyes I have always lacked a certain . . . gravitas, though to be fair to him, Laura, he stepped into the background when he finally realized I'd won you. You were the triumph of my life, Laura.

When I arrived at his club, he was waiting for me, seated in a vast, leather chair, the fingers of one hand drumming impatiently on the arm rest. When I got closer, I realized from his face that this might be the result of tension rather than impatience. He rose to greet me and spoke as abruptly as ever.

"Andrew, thanks for coming. Sit down. Drink?"

"Yes. Whisky, please."

He motioned to a waiter, ordered our drinks and then put an envelope on the side table.

"I want to give you something. I think you need to see it."

Perhaps the secret of Jack Rowden's appeal for women is that his voice is so full of quiet authority that "Will you sleep with me?" must have sounded like an order. How did I ever defy him, Laura, when he begged you to wait . . . not to rush things? Love, Laura. It was love which gave me such courage.

"What is it?"

"It's a diary," he replied.

"Whose diary?"

"Jane's."

"Jane's diary? Why on earth would you give me Jane's diary?"

"Read it. Then you'll understand. I've been defeated. I've tried with the utmost care to point out to her the dangers of the path she's chosen. I know the hours she spends in Laura's old room and obviously I know about the fasting. Arrogantly, I thought I could contain her, guide her. But I've lost her entirely. Over the years Jane and I have negotiated certain . . . rapids, I suppose. She refers to our problems in the diary – notebook, or whatever you want to call it. It's not like any diary I've ever seen. They won't surprise you. No doubt, you've been aware of our difficulties for years. However, this crisis may be insurmountable. There's no question of professional help, she refuses to see anyone. Jane has always been arrogant, intellectually arrogant. She feels she can solve her own problems.''

I remembered ruefully that Jane's academic career had also been more dazzling than mine. And though her route into the Civil Service had been as a PA, she had quickly become a Special Adviser. Occasionally, her tall, severely-dressed form could be glimpsed on news programmes just behind her Minister as he entered or left the Foreign Office building. Some years ago she had taken early retirement. She sat on the board of the local newspaper group and before Laura's illness had considered becoming a magistrate.

''I found the diary,'' he patted the envelope, ''in the top drawer of Laura's old desk. Since her death I'd never entered Laura's room so I suppose Jane felt safe in leaving it there. But last week something made me visit the room and when I saw the diary, open, I broke every rule by which I've lived and I read it. There was also an old letter folded between two pages. It may be yours. But I assure you, it remained unopened. I can't get through to Jane. This is hard to say, Andrew, but I'm worried for you and . . . your friend."

"My friend?"

"Look, this has been a desperately difficult decision to make. It's such a betrayal. But I feel I have no choice. We've always been distant, you and I. I doubt that either of us has any desire to change that. But I feel a certain responsibility . . ." He handed me the envelope. "Please read it. Can you return it to me first thing in the morning? Jane is away at her sister's until Saturday. Bring it yourself to my office, my secretary will see that I get it immediately. It's best if we don't discuss this matter. It's too difficult for us both. However, in doing this despicable thing, I still believe I'm doing my duty. I just hope I don't live to regret it. Goodbye, Andrew. I have to go now."

I stood up and we shook hands awkwardly.

"Goodbye, Jack. I'll read this at home."

"Yes, yes, of course. But remember, first thing in the morning."

"OK. Good night, Jack."

"Goodnight, Andrew." And he was gone.

I did not open the envelope until I was inside my small house in an unfashionable street in Hampstead. It was our first and at Laura's insistence, our only home. I will leave it soon, Laura, and I believe it feels the oncoming rejection.

This house was an outward symbol of certain material differences which always existed between your family and mine, Laura. You were loyal and understanding when I refused help from your father in the purchase of our first home. My own father, a primary school teacher, had little material help to offer.

My father died in the first year of my marriage from the kind of bungled surgery for an ulcer which 'shouldn't happen in this day and age' but which still does. My mother, to my astonishment, sold our old house and with a small cheque from the insurance company moved to live with my eldest sister in Canada. There, she looks after their children while my sister and her husband teach at High School in Vancouver. My parents were always distant and my mother's letter to me after Laura's death was stilted and uncomforting. Though I understood her decision not to attend the funeral – my sister's youngest son had just had an emergency appendectomy – I felt the bonds between us weaken further.

I walked around my empty house reflecting on its

history before I felt ready to invade the mind of the woman whose daughter I had married. What strange twists of fate bring the weaknesses of others to our attention.

Wednesday, March 2nd
How Can It be Spring?

I do not keep the room just as it was. Nothing is just as it was. Such falseness sickens me now. Now, only truth will do. So I will select carefully and coldly, the words, truthful words only, exact in their meaning, which will describe the room.

This was Laura's room. It is not her room now. It is the room which was hers for almost thirty-three years, first as a child, then young woman, then wife, on her visits to us, her longed-for visits. She never came to us as a mother. I thought losing her baby mid-term, when she had waited so long before trying to start a family, would be the hardest thing she would ever have to face in life.

I do not pull blinds or curtains. Nor do I light candles during my visits to this room. Though I will admit to a ritual of profound cleanliness and to one of fasting. These are ascetic, aesthetic choices, not moral, nor psychological, in their origins.

I want to be clean, and I want to be empty. My will, for now I am all will, is honed to such perfection that on entering the room I am, no matter how inconvenient to myself or others, clean and empty.

I sit on an oak chair with a cross carved on its back, which I bought her when she was twelve and she wished, for the first time, to study alone in her room. The chair had once been part of a set in a convent which had been closed down, to merge its pupils with a secular college, in keeping with the fashion of the times. As a set, the chairs did not sell at auction so I, meanly, bargained for one. What would I have done with six convent chairs? No. I was mean. Meanly, I broke the set on which novitiates had sat at Mass to mark their place in the spiritual hierarchy of the convent. Brides to be, of Christ. Later, guiltily, I returned to the convent to buy the rest. But the mother of one of the novitiates had bought a set of four and, just before I arrived, a priest had purchased the last chair. I remember feeling unlucky, and then defiant. The arrogance of the rationalist, who still isn't quite certain.

I remove the chair, the single chair, from its position in front of the wooden desk. I note the budding, polythene-covered magnolia trees sway a little in the wind. They are protected. They will be safely brought to spring. I gaze and see, yet do not see, my own familiar garden. There is no discovery, only unveiling, and it was winter which had revealed the broken column. Your youth and beauty concealed a weakness, Laura, till that December day when we began our journey from a lost Garden of Eden to the Garden of Gethsemane.

When she arrives she takes her place opposite me on a low wooden stool in front of the fireplace. We face each other, I with my back to the window, which I open even in winter, she with her back to the fire. And though she is here I cannot embrace her. I am robbed of her corporeal reality.

I always wait for her to speak. Arrivals and departures are mostly tense, reminders of the first arrival and last departure. My husband, the classicist, the cold classicist, some months ago told me the myth of Demeter, who called forth her daughter Persephone, each year, from the grave. Was he warning me to limit your visits? And last week, he spoke of Ate, who makes men blind, but who has a light touch. This old knowledge does not help me. All knowledge is not good.

I never question her. And I never, ever weep. Often she starts with, "Well . . . well."

"Yes," I answer.

"Does he still visit?"

"Oh, yes."

"Alone?"

"In the beginning."

"And now?"

"Only once with someone else?"

"Who?"

"His cousin. You remember her."

"Her?"

"Yes."

"Ah."

I say nothing. And think of the great good fortune of those who die without knowing how, or when, their child will die. And yet sometimes, I think how terrible to leave with such questions unanswered. Oh, I wasn't born for this, but I'm learning. Being taught to learn.

"Life must go on." She smiles.

"So they say."

"Ridiculous expression. It clearly doesn't. Go on, I mean."

"No."

"It didn't for me."

"No, Laura." I move my face a little to the left. It is a habit when a thought, or word, wounds me suddenly. Such movement does not deflect the blow, but I prefer this angle to a full-face attack.

Silence.

We need to get this part of the conversation over, but the right note must be struck. The words seem to form a poem. It is a poem which will not work with even tiny changes to its rhythm. A casual remark, or a misquotation, can destroy the power of the secret incantation. I concentrate hard. I know to my cost the price of an error. Silence. No sound. No sound whatever. Do you know this no sound? Have you ever heard that kind of silence? I am frightened of no sound, and I am wise to fear it.

"How long is it now?"

"You know."

"Yes, I know. But tell me. I like to count the days of my non-life."

I remain silent. I know she wants not days to be numbered. She thinks to tease me.

She giggles.

"It's not days, is it?"

"No."

"Is it months?"

"Yes."

"But not years."

"No."

"But it will be."

"Yes."

"Oh, yes. Oh, yes."

She starts to laugh. "Life, as they say, must go on."

I gaze straight ahead and hold myself rigid. A line floats back to me . . . 'Queens have died young and fair.'

"Death certainly does, doesn't it? Doesn't it . . . go on?"

The laughter is louder now.

"Unlike life, death goes on and on and on. It's so boring," she screams, "so boring."

I know she lies.

"I'm lying," she says.

"I know."

"But only a little. There is a little truth in it, don't you think? Sorry. I'm so sad. I mock, and then I'm so sad. Do you remember Rosie? The Brannington baby? She keeps singing, though it won't last much longer, I think. She seems to be getting fainter and fainter.''

''Same song?''

''Lullaby. It's a lullaby. You know it's a lullaby. I've told you before it's a lullaby. Try to remember what I tell you. Please try. It's Brahms, 'Seothín Seó'.'' She starts to hum.

''That's Gaelic.''

''I know. And I told you that before. Remember?''

''Well, she won't sing it to the next. . .'' I stop.

''The next? The next,'' she screams.

''The next. Rosie's mother is pregnant again,'' I whisper, frightened.

''Oh, God. Oh, God. What a funny, cruel thing. Another baby, oh poor Rosie. Poor Rosie. She keeps on singing 'Seothín Seó'. It's all she knows. It's all she ever knew. No wonder she's getting fainter. They're beginning to forget. They're beginning to forget Rosie. Poor Rosie. After me? Who's the next? After me? Don't lie to me. Who is the girl?''

''No. No, there is no girl.''

''Don't lie to me,'' she screams again. I shiver. I decide to lie.

"I met him once, with a girl, in the street."

"What's her name?"

Name. Give her a name.

"Sarah. Her name was Sarah."

"Sarah? Sarah. I can hear him, 'Oh, Sarah, Sarah, comfort me, Sarah. Aah.' What does . . . Sarah-Sarah look like?"

"Nice. She looks nice."

"What kind of nice?"

"Kind, nice. That kind."

"Kind? Was I kind?"

"Yes, oh yes."

"I don't remember kind."

"What do you remember most?"

"What I remember most is water. I remember water most."

A letter fell out of the diary and though I recognized my handwriting I felt nothing. So much in life which should shock us simply does not. I picked it up and read it. Any lover's letter to any lover. Love, amore, amour, it's all the same — 'Stay with me. Stay with me. There is something in me . . . that needs something of you . . .'

To my darling Laura,
who lives a twenty-minute swim from me.

Laura, look, look at the way I write your name.
Can you see the line of love, Laura? Laura, lovely
Laura.

I will always remember water. And that I lived a
twenty-minute swim from you.

Tonight, after you had waited for me in the hut
and I wet your dress with my soaking body, you
smiled such a smile, Laura. Oh, Laura, Laura, I
will never forget your smile as you stood there in
your wet silky dress. And then you lay down and I
felt as though I swam up and down your body,
Laura. And that the movements you made were like
those of the fish, hidden and quick. And then our
laughter splashed about us, Laura. And oh, Laura, I
will never forget your laughter.

And later, when you walked away and gave me
your salute, your hands locked above your naked
arms which stretched to the sky, you seemed to sway
in the wind. Oh, Laura.

When I got home my parents were waiting. I hid
my trunks in the pocket of my jacket, but they
knew where I had been. They said nothing. I think
they were frightened of me. I'm glad. Then as I put

my jacket on the back of the chair my trunks fell out. They made a tiny splash of water, which seemed like a shallow mirror on the floor. And I tried to cup it up, because of you. I felt you were hiding, somewhere in the water.

I stared at them and as I put my swimming trunks back in my pocket I was certain I could defy them in anything. I thought of you, Laura, and I made a promise to you that I would never be weak. Time waits for me, Laura, and it wants to watch me soar. I am now at the beginning of the arc and I must fly higher. For I have won you, Laura. And then I started to laugh. I couldn't help myself. It started deep inside me and cascaded over me like water, like a torrent and I carried my parents along with my laughter.

Later, when I fell asleep I dreamed of you, my tall, athletic goddess on the hill, as I grew smaller and smaller, till I became the fish.

I'm writing this at five in the morning. There is a fog over the lake and I feel as though I could walk through the fog, to you, Laura. I know this letter seems strange. I'm trying to write like Keats! I feel like Keats and that you are my Fanny. But oh, how I prefer your name, Laura, Laura, Laura,

Laura, who lives a twenty-minute swim from me.
Laura, of the smile I will never forget.
Laura, of the laughter I will never forget.
Laura, Laura, Laura . . . .

LAURA, I love you,
Andrew

And I felt nothing. Absolutely nothing. I turned to the next page of the diary.

Thursday, March 10th

Sometimes my darling, lost daughter, Laura Bolton, née Rowden, only stays for minutes. I have no gift to hold her. It is a power I lost long ago. Powerlessness is what I learn daily. Maybe in time to come, if there is time to come, when time, for me, comes to an end, I will remember powerlessness most. As she remembers water.

I too remember water and I remember him as a boy – young man – I suppose. I remember him dripping, Shelley-like, as he strode towards her. Leaving an image of himself from which she could never escape. Only half-knowing and not in his brain but in his body, how powerful he would always be.

The boy, Andrew Bolton, who came to her dripping, to his worship and seduction. Never one, without the other. Oh, I remember water too and their letters which I found that summer, when we knew we couldn't stop them. And when the boy hit back and raged against us, as boys in their lust will always hit back at whoever tries to stop them. Who can ever stop them?

Well, she had that, I suppose. Sometimes I tell myself that was everything and sometimes I listen and believe. And yet when I see her childhood friend, solid, three-dimensional, gaily-clothed, and now pregnant, plodding through a haze of hope to motherhood, I could run and scream at her. And then I stop and think, it's not her fault.

I have taught myself to love my husband, Jack, again — at least a little. A lesson for which I am grateful. He stayed with me through the time I spent dreaming of Austen Duffield. He waited for me through the time, shorter, that I spent with Austen Duffield. The six weeks which taught me the limitations of my courage. Over the years, my husband's infidelities had broken the circle, they had left him defenceless. Stunned at how defenceless he was, Jack waited for me. And he tried his best to please me, though we both knew I pleased him not. And his other women soothed him and hoped for more from him. But he waited for me. While he loved women, I loved one man. And it wasn't him. He waited it out. I give him credit for that.

Saturday, sometime in April
Went Shopping. What For?

"Good morning, Mrs Peters." Surely shopping in the village is an innocent pastime.

"Good morning, Mrs Rowden." Mrs Peters smiles back at me, still a little wary, in case I might stop and talk. And then talk of the reality which Mrs Peters wishes into unreality.

I pass on. I have no desire to burden Mrs Peters with anything. And besides, I do not always carry my burden. Sometimes, Mrs Peters, I leave it at home. Sometimes, dear Mrs Peters, I climb the body of Austen Duffield. You remember him, Mrs Peters? He came to the village, to dispose of his uncle's property, Cornhill Manor. Well, Mrs Peters, I dream my mouth is on his stomach now. Did you ever want to climb a man, Mrs Peters? The way one climbs a mountain? To stretch along the ground and touch his feet and move up his body. I was born to hold my face beneath his foot and not feel fear. You see, Mrs Peters, we dream of both the living and the dead. And very little is real.

"Mrs Rowden."

I turn around. "Yes."

Mrs Peters has come back towards me.

"I wanted to say so much at the time. But I just couldn't. I wanted you to know . . . how . . . how deeply sorry we were. We wrote, of course, but . . ."

"I understand. Thank you. Thank you."

I suppose you think that enough time has passed now, Mrs Peters. I suppose you think my face looks different now. Does it look normal, Mrs Peters? And normal is different from how it was. Isn't that right? I am now, once again, back in the land of the living – as they say. Back in the land of the living now, Mrs Peters. I must touch something solid or I'll be lost again. I touch a railing and lean on it. Mrs Peters' face is frightened. She thinks I'm going to faint. I must reassure her, so I laugh. My husband, who stayed with me after I'd climbed all over another man, my husband Jack, calls it my high, singing laugh. Shall I give her some facts? Mrs Peters knows so few facts. There are so few facts. But death is one of them. It is pure fact. And we long so for decoration. Sex we can decorate. Oh, yes. Sex begets us and death ends us. And in between? It depends on how long in between is, Mrs Peters. The tough old story of the world.

"Mrs Peters, my new shoes are so uncomfortable. Would you hold my bag for me? Just for a moment, while I ease them a little?"

"Of course, of course." Mrs Peters beams at me. She is happy to be of help. Oh, joy for Mrs Peters. I am not going to break her day into pieces of grief. And Mrs Peters believes she has been of some real use to me, in my discomfort, my false discomfort, in my poor betrayed-by-lies shoes. She's soothed now and tentatively she speaks, "God, they say, Mrs Rowden, fits the back to the burden." "Oh, fuck off, Mrs Peters. Fuck off." Silently.

We part. The gaiety's gone. I'm tired. I'll go home now. The noise in the street is unbearable. At home I will have silence. Until my husband returns.

Perhaps? Perhaps she's there?

I walk into the room. The room that was hers. But I am not clean. I am not empty. She does not come.

May Day
Dressing and Undressing the Body

Jack and I went to a dinner party. I have lost more weight. But what is haggard in daylight can look chic at night. I wore a black suit and a pearl choker. It was not original but I knew I looked impressive.

Jack does not flirt in my presence but there was a woman there who interested him. I can always tell. She was wearing green. I felt no envy. Someone on my right bored me with details of his success, 'I smile, of course, and go on drinking' . . . wine.

When we got home I knew the woman in the green dress had not captured his imagination. Was that sad for her? I often think of them – the others – and want to say, "I know he's good. I know he does it well. Enjoy it. I couldn't give a damn."

I was slightly drunk, in my own way, which is quietly and full of violence, which is hidden.

I fuck my husband. I have never been sentimental about sex. There is passion or pleasure – sometimes there is passion and pleasure. Tonight was expert, quick and a little brutal – exactly as I wanted. Later, when he was asleep (the Samson syndrome – forget the hair, he was exhausted from sex) I left the bed and seemed to drift towards Laura's room hoping for

a night visit. As I crossed the balcony I let my slip fall
from my body. I loathe nightdresses or pyjamas and I
walked into the room naked. In a mirror I glimpsed
my angular shape, long and severe, with small breasts.
This woman is wearing well, I thought, because there
is little to droop or become unpleasingly soft.

It is cold. I like that. The wooden chair is
unyielding. Good. I demand you come to me, Laura.
I'm drunk, Laura. Will you notice? I wait. I am
determined. After a time . . .

"I never saw you naked, Mother. Why?"

"Oh, it happened. Perhaps you were too young to
remember."

"And later?"

"I don't know. What a strange thing nakedness is.
How it disturbs us, Laura. I remember once when
you were too ill to walk to the bathroom your father
carried you and I took off your nightdress and he
placed you gently in the bath. And you wept and
wept as though you were ashamed that he had seen
you naked. Afterwards he carried you, wrapped in a
towel, to your room. I loved him terribly that day.
Do you remember that nakedness, Laura? I remember."

"Oh God, please go away now, Mother. I want to cry for the body I once had. And I want to cry alone."

What could I say? I returned to bed, to my husband, to the body I knew so well, to its sounds, odours, movements and its nakedness.

June 14th

'Fare Forward'. Why Not? At Least For Two Hours . . .

I went to the quarterly Board Meeting of the newspaper group. I have missed two. Everyone understood. They played the game knowing only its surface rules.

I wore red, a pillar-box red suit and bright red lipstick. I looked, as they say, 'bloody but un-bowed'. Did anyone wish to hose me down?

"Gentlemen. Jane, Jane, it's so good to see you back with us."

"Looking magnificent, if I may say so, Jane."

"Jack all right?"

"Well. He's very well, Alexander. Thank you. Thank you all."

"Right. Shall we begin? No apologies, glad to say." Alexander smiled at me encouragingly. "Minutes of the Last Meeting . . ."

Minutes of the Last Meeting

The house is empty. I wait outside your room, I sense that you will call to me. I'm tired. How much time has passed? I lie on the floor, supplicant, and gaze at the ceiling, watching visions of you, Laura, like clouds in the sky creating unreliable patterns that race and then are still and then bundle one on top of the other and, like you, are there and then are not there.

Are you there, my lovely girl? Are you there in your room? May I come in, may I enter, darling girl? No one answers. I push the door and call to you.

"I want to be with you, Laura." I sense her weeping in the corner.

"Let me comfort you, Laura. I want to comfort you."

"I want? I want. I used to say that a lot, Mother. I want you to go. I promise next time will be better."

The weeping ceased and I sat alone, sweating in the cold room.

Thursday, July 28th
Andrew Rang. Sometimes I hate him.

"Come. Of course, Andrew. Come, make it early. We can have a walk in the garden." Just voices on the phone. Mine, and the husband she had, once. The faces are mercifully hidden.

"Yes, I'd like that, Jane."

"You'll be alone?"

"Of course."

Of course. But you're not always alone any more, are you, Andrew? How many women by now, how many women? It's a kind of adultery. Adds to the thrill, perhaps. Sinless adultery yet with an aspect of betrayal. Spices it up I suppose. My language has changed. I prefer the word cunt to vagina and fuck to intercourse. I'm still puritanical about the others. I have a short, silent monologue. It goes like this. "Fuck you, life," over and over again, "Fuck you, life."

"Jane?"

"Yes. Sorry, Andrew — my mind wanders a little."

"Shall I come at twelve-thirty — or is that too early?"

"No. That's perfect."

" 'Bye then."

"Goodbye."

Goodbye.

'Good-night, ladies; good-night sweet ladies; good-night, good-night.'

Good-night, sweet lady, to whom once, long ago, I taught that line.

First Sunday in August
Andrew Comes to Lunch. He Looks Well. He Looks Too Well.

"How are you, Jane?" He kisses me. The man who so often kissed her and now kisses other women that way, the way that tells you everything. I'm sure by now he kisses other women. The body has its own timetable and does not always wait for the heart. Maybe I'm wrong. Maybe, as yet, he kisses no one that way, the other way, so different from the way he kisses me, the mother of the woman he loved and then married and then lost. Lost? Why do we use that word when it implies such cruel possibilities?

He is a handsome man. Too slight for me but then he was not destined for me. He has the languid elegance that is an extra gift to those who are both tall and thin. I do not respond sexually to those men whose bodies cannot dominate mine, an out-of-fashion desire.

Well, tell him how you are.

"I'm well, Andrew, quite well." Not that I care.

Later

How Can a Day be so Long?

Andrew asked about Jack, whom I know he hates. Why are people such liars?

I'd read somewhere – or had Claud told me? – that he was to interview Catherine Samuelson. When I mentioned it, he just couldn't hide his pride. Life, they say, they always say, must go on. Fuelled particularly by the ego. Good old ego, how maligned you are. Good old pride, sends something of life surging through the veins. Something to keep the heart beating.

When he said, "I'm surprised, of course, that Catherine Samuelson agreed," I almost laughed. He had never sounded surprised by good fortune. Andrew was always a little too certain, until all certainties ended. But it's coming back. A kind of certainty. For him.

He smiled suddenly, perhaps through embarrassment. I hate his smile now. That smile which won her. It is so total, and so totally resembled hers. When they stood before us, Laura and Andrew, with their twinned smiles of almost insane joy, we knew we had lost. But we knew nothing of loss then. Nothing.

We went for a walk before lunch. Autumn had been the first season, after. I had noticed everything more keenly and felt it slightly cruel to crush the leaves, having, for a short time, a different relationship with the earth.

I thought of how his future would push you down the well of memory and finally, flood you out, Laura. You would become a faint echo of another life. My darling daughter, you will be like the flash of colour in the lake when the fish shimmers to the surface, just to prove it can at will intrude on our world and, at will, disappear. Perhaps he will have children. They will not be yours, Laura. They will not be my grandchildren. No grandchildren for me.

Perhaps, for everyone's sake, I should not encourage him to come to see us. As soon as that thought came to me, I rejected it. I told him how much we wanted to see him. Am I lying? I don't know what I think from minute to minute.

Then, suddenly – so suddenly – he said, "I've met a girl, a young woman."

"That's natural." What else could I say? But so soon.

And then he said, "Her name's Sarah." And I nearly cried out, "Oh, God. Sarah."

"Is it serious?"

When he said, "I don't know," I knew it must be. When they don't know, it means it's serious.

"I wanted to tell you before anyone . . ." he seemed almost angry in his embarrassment.

"Told me?"

"Yes. It seemed right that I should. You know, when you're in town you might hear something . . ."

"You're kind to tell me." What can I say or do?

I had forgotten how young he is. A young man's body. The body I worshipped, Austen's body, was older, heavier and not so elegant. Would they have remained together, I wonder? Would he have remained faithful? Or, would she have found, older, as I did, something fierce she had not known before? They were not fierce together. Strange how rarely young love is.

"She's worked for the past six months on *After Words*. That's how we met. She does research."

Oh God, another cliché. Why couldn't she have climbed the Andes, or been a poet, or something wild? So, daughter, you died and he met a researcher on his programme. And oh, he'll probably marry her. He's a lazy loaf, your husband. They'll have children. That's really how you will have shaped his life and hers, Laura. You will have contributed to Sarah's life, a husband, yours.

I have a desperate need to see this Sarah and asked him to bring her here to lunch. He almost shouted, "No. No, I couldn't do that." And I knew then that we would slip away. Sarah would make it happen. I don't blame her. "It's for your own good," she'll tell him. "Better this way. We must move on."

'Move on over', daughter. After all, you have 'passed away'. You have 'left us'. As though you had a choice. More and more, I become angry with those who commit suicide. 'Is it the way out or the way in?' Who was my husband quoting? You are, sweet child, 'no longer with us'. You are dead. 'but that was in another country, and besides, the wench is dead.' I know now why those lines will last forever.

The lunch petered out, and as he left we both

regretted it. It had not worked. He will be wary of trying again. Sarah will not, I fear, encourage him. I did not ask him if he would stop to visit your grave, Laura. It is an impossible question, an unforgivable intrusion. God, this landscape is a minefield. Everyone trying to avoid the word or deed, that might lead to some explosion of grief. An explosion which wounds bystanders, which is why they fear it so. Others' tears are a kind of emotional shrapnel, that may scar. He waved, blew a kiss of sorts, and was gone. Perhaps to Sarah. Or perhaps he stopped for a visit, my dear child, on the way.

Shall I follow? Shall I follow him and watch him hesitate for a moment, uncertain and disturbed . . . then, foot on accelerator, speed away, racing through his time, after yours had ended. 'The charming church and churchyard situated just outside the village is definitely worth a visit. Then have tea in Mrs Gantry's Copper Kettle. Or in summer watch cricket on the green. England . . . so much remains to enchant and delight.' Thus runs the old guide book which I still keep after all these years.

In all those years, how few funerals we had attended in our local churchyard. How rarely did I watch the merciless hiding of the wooden treasure chest in the ground – buried treasure – yet not marked with skull and crossbones, at last appropriate in this place. Though personal taste determines how the spot is marked, few are innovative in the decoration of the grave. No. My memory is of metropolitan services, so sane, so calm, occasionally even chic. No one ever screamed. I do remember that, and wonder now why no one ever screamed.

No, he will not visit today and neither will I. I no longer weep there and that is hard. In truth, I rarely weep now, knowing that it is useless. Tears are a release of rage or bitterness, or an expression of despair or exhaustion. But in the end you, or someone else, must dry them and nothing has been changed. Once, I wept for my own way and got it. Or wept for succour of a kind and got it. I have wept tears of jealousy, tears of rejection. Oh, I've run the whole gamut of tears. And it is only now that I know their inappropriateness to the great moments of life.

Sarah, Sarah. What is her second name? I want to see this Sarah. It is the first thing I have wanted for a long time. I am excited by the desire to see this girl. If she were his mistress when he was married to you, Laura, would I have wanted to see her then? I would. But I would have been too afraid of you. You terrified us all with your sudden angers. But now you are dead, Laura. Now you are powerless. Now I can do as I want. I have the ruthlessness of the living.

Friday, August 19th
Dictation

I am clever. I decided to ring Claud, the watcher from the wings in my marriage. Every marriage has one. As a result of a recent take-over, Claud is now also MD of the company which produces Andrew's programmes. When he took over, he moved some of his old team with him. I remember that Andrew was worried for a while. How unlike Andrew.

I made a short list of questions. I have to be careful with Claud, he's such a highly-strung man. A few years ago marriage problems seemed to totally overwhelm him . . . some girl we never knew. It's all over now I gather. "We see each other often. We're friends. She's a nice girl . . ." That was his last and final comment. We didn't question him. Our friendship, though old, has strict limitations.

I had a pen and paper beside me as we spoke. My old skills came back to me from the time when I started in the Civil Service and met my brilliant husband-to-be.

Claud sounded as uncomfortable as always with me. But he had usually been around when I needed him. Why, I'd often wondered. Loyalty to Jack, with whom he had been at Oxford? Reporting back, to my husband, on how I was 'taking it'? My husband Jack, whose over-educated, over-disciplined mind made him a Treasury guru and whose libidinous pursuits occasionally caused genuine alarm.

"Andrew came to lunch the other day." I started the conversation.

"I know, he told me."

"Looks well. I thought."

"Not bad, not bad. Considering."

"He seems really pleased and excited about this Catherine Samuelson interview."

"Well, it's quite a coup. It's good for his career."

"When does it shoot?"

"Oh, October, I think."

"Is he with his old team? I mean, everything changes so fast now in TV. No old teams left."

"No." I hear the hesitation in his voice.

"He told me about Sarah, Claud. Don't be

embarrassed." Always best, with Claud, to come straight to the point.

"Did he? I didn't know there was much to tell."

"Do you know her?"

A hesitation.

"Well, do you know her?"

"Yes. A little. I don't think this is wise, do you, Jane? There are bound to be women, you know."

"I like the plural, Claud. Makes me feel better about Laura's singular position as wife. At least for now. Don't worry, I do realize that eventually he'll marry again."

"Yes, I suppose he will."

"Someone else will think he was her destiny. All that was required was Laura's death. Isn't that strange? Did you like her?"

"Who?" Claud sounded almost angry with embarrassment.

"Laura. Did you like her?" I persisted.

"My God, I'd known her since she was a child. Of course I liked her."

"Why are you so distressed? Because her mother asks these questions? Or because she's dead?"

"I'm sorry, Jane. I just still can't believe it's happened."

You can't rehearse this role. It's a secret text, not handed down from generation to generation. The church buries young and old in the same way. And gives no guidance at all. Natural and unnatural deaths elicit the same memorial service.

"Though I'm her mother and I loved her deeply, I didn't always like her, Claud. I thought she could be cold when she didn't get her own way. Did you ever think her cold?"

"No. Not really. She was sometimes reserved with me." And I thought, it's true. Apart from that glorious smile and the sudden tempers, Laura was, in a way, reserved. I wonder would you have been less reserved, Laura, had you known how little time you had? How short your reserved life would be. And now you are abandoned by that life about which you were once so reserved. I must stop talking about you. Claud can't take much more. And you, Laura, cannot interrupt us.

"Tell me about the girl. Twenty questions? That old game, remember, Claud? When I asked you about the other women?"

"Yes, I remember."

"Play the game, Claud."

"This is all wrong."

"Please, Claud?"

"Oh, all right."

"Looks?"

"Average."

"Height?"

"Average, maybe a bit above. God, I don't know
— I suppose she's tallish."

"Figure?"

"Average."

"Oh, all right. She's an all-round average girl."

"Yes."

"You don't want to talk about her, do you?"

"No, I don't want to talk about her."

"Why?"

A long pause. Claud seems even more careful than
usual.

"Because your interest is unhealthy . . ."

"How do you know it's not much worse, actually
malevolent?"

"You're not a malevolent woman."

Is he right? "But there's no virtue here, Claud. I'm
not malevolent because I know it's useless."

"You must leave the girl alone. Leave him alone.
Your relationship with him is different now."

"It's less. Everything is less. It's so cruel. Not just the loss of her. But less of everything."

"I know."

"Do you?"

"Yes, Jane. I do."

I didn't ask how, and I abruptly said goodbye. I am too weak to bear another's pain. I want to concentrate on my own. The selfishness of the newly bereaved. No one has suffered as I have. Take this pain away. It is not for me, this bitter cup. Damn you. Don't force me to drink it. Aargh. There, there. It's all finished. To the dregs. Well done. Good girl. You drank it to the dregs. That's the best way, believe me. All this business of little sips and everyone holding your hand. A total waste of time. Open your mouth. Let the lava in. Down the tongue and throat it goes, stripping the membrane. Good, everything will sound and taste different. As it should. But that's life, dear. That's what death does to life, it burns a new pattern on the body, a tattoo of loss. Internal and external loss, etched in acid on your soul, on mind, on memory, wherever the hell you think the real you resides. Where, oh where, does the real you reside, Laura? Tell me where? And I shall join you. But where? 'What happens to the living

when they die? Death is not understood by death: nor
you, nor I.' I read those lines last week and learned
them by heart. For tomorrow, the first anniversary.

Thursday, September 8th
Her Face. At First from a Distance.

When I first saw them together, Andrew and Sarah,
walking out of the TV studios, I was not, as I had
expected, pierced by anguish. Of course, I had been
waiting for them, in my strategically parked car. And
I had made preparations, which always lessens pain. I
had already painted on my mind's eye a female body,
that would walk beside his and link her arm in his.
You, the original woman, Laura, had been rubbed
out. The way a child vigorously rubs away the error
he has made, and then, pleased with himself and
blowing the bread-like crumbs across the surface of
the page, starts again, more carefully. Just a little over
a year ago, had any arm been on his, so intimately,
had any face looked at his, so warmly, had any mouth
seduced him, it would have been yours, Laura. But
they are gone. Your arms, your face, your mouth are
gone. They are boxed in wood, earth pushing at the
sides. And though I cannot bear to think of it, I

suppose life, of sorts, tries to creep its way towards you, and I hope still fails.

I started my car and drove away. It was enough. I had had the first blurred sighting of the about-to-be-permanent couple. My son-in-law's new companion who will, no doubt, be his wife. Let's play with the sound, Sarah Bolton. It sounds right. It sounds good, solid. Better than Laura Bolton? No, no, you couldn't say that. But let's be fair, it sounds good.

My husband will not be told of this little activity of mine. My new way of passing time; though time needs no help to pass. For he would quote something, or tell me some story from antiquity and I might just hate him. And I have little energy for that now. We do not live soul to soul. We never have. I could have told Austen, he would have understood. But I lost Austen. I lacked courage. I wanted to protect my life. Ha, to protect my life. And having protected my life, this is what waited for me down the road. Life, I now know, has a way of testing the fault line, as though conducting a scientific experiment.

And you, Laura, will never see Sarah. The Sarah who will step into her new life as your replacement. Shall I tell you, Laura, the story of how life went on, when I talk to you, if you come to your empty room, in my empty house? No, perhaps I won't tell you. Perhaps this is just something else you will never know.

Tuesday, 27th
Only Women Bleed

I saw your replacement next by accident, Laura. I was driving towards the TV studio, working out a better place to park in order to spy on them, your husband and his 'new friend'. I have become more fearless in words and in actions. I now say to spy, not to observe. I tell myself fewer lies. Oh dear, where will all this truthfulness end? She wore a long beige raincoat, flat shoes and carried a large, brown, leather bag. Her light-coloured hair was held back in a band. She has long legs. Sarah is even leggier than you were, Laura. I parked quickly and followed her into the shop.

What would she buy? Hurriedly, she bought tampons. And I started to cry. I knew I would not have wept over lipstick, scarves or books but tampons moved me to sudden tears. And all that was between us, Laura, in our female world, came surging back to me. Your little skinniness and embarrassed pride, when we talked of what would happen to your body, and when I suspended, just, the disbelief that the long, straight lines of your body would change, that the creamy skin would be covered with down, then hair, and that you, like me, would bleed. And I remembered the song that shocked me so with its explicitness – 'Only Women Bleed'.

And when it happened, at your friend Maria's house, as luck would have it, you sobbed to me over the phone to come and take you home. You would not let me ask Maria's mother, Pamela, to give you sanitary towels, crying "No, no, take me home." Then whispering, "I don't want anyone to know." And though I think Pamela guessed, poor little Maria looked puzzled and upset. We stopped on the way home and I bought you small-size pads. I was grateful that you did not need the hideous belts I wore when I was young to hold the pad in place. Now, a strip of adhesive could position the pad in your knickers. Crying, you went to the bathroom and emerged a bleeding young female with the anguished face of a child of five. And my heart felt broken in some way, knowing your childhood was gone forever. I kept your secret. In the beginning, you were certain your father could not possibly know of such things. And you refused to explain the sudden way you grabbed your stomach when the cramps came. And he, being in so many ways a very nice man, Laura, never said a word. He never acknowledged in all your teenage years that you had ever had a period. I loved you so desperately that sodden day. Where, oh where have you gone, child?

I wanted to sink to my knees in the shop as Sarah – perhaps soon to be Bolton – paid for her tampons. I wanted to sink to my knees and never move again. Just to beat the floor with my fists until someone would come and take me away. But one doesn't do such things. And as I stood there she turned suddenly and bumped into me. "Oh, I'm so sorry, I do apologize." I must have stared at her strangely or perhaps she saw my tears, for she said, "Oh, God, did I hurt you? How clumsy of me, I'm so clumsy." I felt my tears come again. I shook my head. "No, no, it's OK. I'm sorry," and I walked away.

When I turned around she had gone. She had left with her tampons. A young woman, surprised as women often are, by the erratic nature of blood.

I put the diary to one side and wondered: what is

expected of me here? What does Jack want me to do? What can be done? Warn Sarah? But of what? Bring Jane and Sarah together? No. Impossible. But why not? Maybe that is the best course.

Then I felt angry. I had been invaded. I did not want to know these things. Is this Jack's revenge on me?

I thought of how defeated we all were, and with that defeat came profound uncertainty. We, who had been so certain of everything. Particularly Jack, who had always managed his wife, his mistresses, and his Treasury Department. Jack, who had a quote from antiquity for everything, was now uncertain in his own grief how to react to the extreme agony of his wife, and like the messenger in some Greek tragedy, he ran from a house of sorrow with grave tidings of further wrath to come.

I returned the diary the following morning:

Jack,
Laura's mother will never do harm in Laura's name.
Uncertain as I now am about everything in life —
uncertain as we all are — this I know to be true.

When the Catherine Samuelson interview is
finished, I will try to bring Jane and Sarah
together. I have a feeling this will help. The last
entry in the diary is much less angry than the first.

So I'm very hopeful.

In the meantime, there was a nurse at the hospice, I found her number, 0181 644 6508 — I remember Jane found her extremely helpful in those last days.

Finally, I know this has been very, very difficult for you. I am profoundly grateful,

Yours,
Andrew.

SIX

"She's said no to the ICA and the National. Evidently she had some row with 'Sir' once, and has never forgotten it. So, it's only you, before the first preview."

Drinks with my producer, Brian Grearson. Same pub as of old, same man, same jokey mannerisms, same casual, unstructured and expensive uniform, everything's the same. And I remembered how to be.

"Incidentally, I've heard that Francis Byfleet is writing an unauthorized biography. I gather she's furious. I've got the article he wrote about her last year."

"I'm sure it's in the file Sarah's preparing for me."

"Well, here's a copy. It begins with 'She was my father's mistress.' Amazing chap, Byfleet. Do you want to talk to him?"

"No, he's all vitriol."

"Still, it might be worth trying to get his point of view."

"I understand his point of view on most matters. God, we're subjected to it every week in *The Sunday Chronicle*. It's just that I detest it."

"Well, at least that's a refreshing bit of passion from you. Haven't seen much of that . . ."

I let the silence make its own comment, and thought that small angers could suddenly engulf me in a way that small joys never did.

"Sorry, Andrew, that was meant to sound different. Came out the wrong way."

I shook my head. "Everything anyone says comes out the wrong way. I don't have a right way of listening."

"Time," he said.

"Yes, of course, time."

"Here, take the article. I've got to dash. Have a quick look. Let's talk tomorrow."

"Thanks. Goodbye, Brian." I ordered another drink and started to read.

The Wrong Truth and Catherine Samuelson
by Francis Byfleet

In the manner of today, I must at least imply a form of intellectual integrity by declaring an interest. Catherine Samuelson was my father's mistress.

If that was all Catherine Samuelson had been, neither I, nor anyone else, would wish to write about her. She is, of course, a noted playwright – author of twelve plays, a much-discussed and admired artist.

Catherine Samuelson, artist, destroyed a family ... a commonplace tragedy. Grand passion, like great art, often leaves in its wake innocent victims. It must, in fairness, be noted how easily the victim surrenders, perhaps mesmerized by a power they have been long taught to worship. Does their weeping matter? Not a jot, I hear you say. If the artist adds to the canon, he or she has added to that essential spiritual bank on which all mankind can call. If only to prove the importance of the species. Art is a god. Gods require sacrifice. It is interesting to note how rarely the artist is sacrificed and how often an acolyte is called upon to play his, or her, thankless part.

Catherine Samuelson has always been desperately interested in 'doing good' in the lives of those she does not know. Are we entitled to test the rhetoric against the life? To which I answer an emphatic yes. Otherwise, what was the rhetoric for? Did you harm those around you? Or were your ideals held strictly in reserve for strangers?

Catherine Samuelson is in love with chaos. She

fiinds 'something rotten' in the organized state, everywhere. Only revolution is pure. She seems to ignore the fact that stability is a hard-won thing, that even a flawed democracy is to be treasured. Valhalla, if you believe in heaven, comes only after death.

Many members of Miss Samuelson's family died in the Holocaust. This is a fact to which she rarely, if ever, refers, refusing to feed what she describes as 'minds greedy for horror'. Her simple statement: 'Six million people were massacred during Nazi Germany's persecution of the Jews. Religion failed to stop this evil. Diplomacy failed to stop it. Art was irrelevant. Only war ended it. We must learn, punish and remember,' has a certain grave authority. But something is missing. Humility perhaps?

Her later, notorious remark about the Holocaust: 'In this the Jews behaved like Christians', managed to alienate both Christians and Jews. Angry, she punished us, as she would see it, by not writing for six years. It was during those years that she met my father, Arthur Byfleet, and began the affair which so devastated our family and with which I will deal at greater length in my forthcoming biography. Miss Samuelson's anger at my threatened 'intrusion' into her private life has been forcefully conveyed to my publishers. Perhaps she should remember that we had no warning and no protection when she 'intruded' on ours.

During her silent years she was Visiting Director at both the Berliner Ensemble and the Moscow Arts Theatre. The tension between the Naturalism of the latter and the didactic approach of the former, particularly in relation to Brecht's famous A-effect, ALIENATION, was, I'm afraid, not beneficial to her subsequent writing. Her later addiction to Beckett-style monologues proved only that she had a good ear for others' genius. Though she is regarded by many as an important playwright, it is my opinion that while she is thematically consistent, she has never found an individual style either as a writer or as a director.

Miss Samuelson has written twelve plays. Though lately she has collaborated with other directors, she directed all her own early work. The first three plays, which formed her trilogy *The Living Truth*, brought her immediate recognition. Then in the early seventies came *Moments of Madness*, *The Void*, *Aaron Masters* and *Beyond Language*. The following decade produced another trilogy, eccentrically titled *Quarto*, and two neo-classical-style plays, *The Gate* and *The Mourning Site*.

But it was her 50s trilogy, *The Living Truth*, which made her name. It served notice of the position from which she has, as yet, never departed, that of destroyer of certain mythologies, as she describes them, on which many people base their lives: the mythology of personality; the mythology of grief; the mythology of the after-life.

Each play in the trilogy examined (I use the term in its medical sense) a family, one in post-Nazi Germany, one in the late '40s in England and one in New York. And each play had an identical opening scene. The characters wakened, the parents had sex, the children had breakfast, then all left for school, or work. With a kind of hypnotic rhythm one ritual followed another, broken only by small 'explosions', in which various characters tried for different reasons to break away. Through the resolution of these tensions it became clear that The Family insidiously imposes unity. Children were subtly manipulated for their own good, to a common mode of action. Their rebellions were unoriginal and in fact only cemented them in their group psychology. Miss Samuelson's main point – that the family is a gang, with its own leader and is a model for the army – was at the time quite controversial and Miss Samuelson became a kind of guru.

There then followed a devastating analysis of *Moments of Madness* and of *Beyond Language*. Bored by their vicious tone I skipped to a kinder appraisal of *The Gate* and *The Mourning Site* and then on to the last paragraphs.

Because of Miss Samuelson's determined following of Brecht – other than in the two neo-classical plays – the audience often leaves the theatre robbed of the normal comfort of drama, catharsis. They are also filled with a kind of contempt for themselves. Meeting Miss Samuelson, as I have so often, they would find that she is inclined to the belief that they are right. This is why her plays are sometimes interesting but not great. And why she fascinates but does not invite affection.

'The Living Truth' about Miss Samuelson is that she herself is, of course, simply one of a gang, as I am sure she would be the first to admit. The gang of 'Robber Artists' I shall call them. They take from us the beliefs on which we build our lives and give us in return the questionable blessing of a savage rage at everything.

We should raise a small, ice-cold vodka to Miss Samuelson, take one sip and move on to a full-bodied wine.

SEVEN

Down each side of a white, narrow, gallery-like room, ran ten rows of wooden benches. Flat, dark cushions added minimal comfort. Two white lines, almost like those on a tennis court, warn the audience — so far and no further. The acting space, a ribbon of polished wood, lay between ranks of benches. There was no escape for either audience or actors.

A young man heard my footsteps and turned around, "Who's there?"

"Sorry — just looking."

"Well, it's not allowed. Who are you? How did you get in?"

"I spoke to the man at the . . ."

"No one's allowed in here until the performance."

"God, are you always this rude?"

"Rude? This is my theatre."

"I thought for the moment it was Catherine Samuelson's."

"You know exactly what I mean. Anyway, what do you want?"

"Nothing. I'm just leaving. I wanted to see the theatre."

"Never been before?" His tone softened, slightly. "It's where she always presents her plays in London. She's a genius."

"Really?"

"Absolutely. This is the experience of a lifetime."

Lifetime. Life time. My relationship with words has changed. It has become intense, frightened. Certain words seem now to attack me, wind me even. And so I try to drown them quickly in a torrent of other words. The air is unfairly, unnecessarily, disturbed. Looking at the young man, I knew from his face that he was innocent of finality. Last act, final curtain, is all he knows of the end of things.

Say something to the young man who is having the experience of a lifetime.

"She's much admired."

"Bloody well ought to be."

"But not by everyone."

"No one who matters a damn is ever admired by everyone."

"Perhaps not."

"Anyway, you still haven't told me who you are." He looked at me properly and he didn't recognize me. I explained myself — inelegantly.

"Well, did I say anything awful? Not that I care, except about her."

"No. You said nothing wrong. You were perfect." Suddenly, an echo. How often did I answer, "You are perfect, Laura" to your cry, "How do I look?" Oh, I could never see a fault in you. For every imperfection was yours and therefore just another aspect of you to worship. Knowing this, I knew everything. It is a heavy burden, this knowledge and I will never unlearn it. And everything else that I will ever learn will be impregnated by that knowledge. Impregnated. I had made you pregnant. Stopped a monthly clock dead, killing one rhythm, to start another. The child didn't come. Why? Perhaps a wise child. How can I say that? What became of us, Laura and Andrew, who once thought our every dream was ours alone? A man, a dead wife and children who never came. Tick tock. Tick tock.

The young man was talking again.

"Nothing's perfect in life. Because the future might

spoil it. That's why people go to the theatre. They want to know the end of the story."

"Surely that's why they read books?"

"Not the same thing. Doesn't look like life, you know?"

"How did you meet her?"

"Oh, after a stint at the National I'd established a bit of a reputation. Then I had a breakdown. She traced me to a mental hospital, a dump really. Since then I've been with her, and I'll stay for as long as she needs me. We're already talking about the next production, *The Mourning Site*, in Warsaw. I've found my world and I'm never fucking leaving it. That's what people should do, don't you think? When they've found their world, never, ever leave it?"

I didn't make the obvious point. If you wait, people always follow through. That's my main skill as an interviewer. Silence. I used to count, one, two, three, maximum eight beats and they'd start again, "What I mean is . . ."

No one prepared me for your permanent silence, Laura. No one told me what endless silence means. Now I listen to silence knowing the beat is forever one, two, three . . . silence, ongoing.

"Well done, Sean. You're getting there."

This is a voice that doesn't often praise, and knows that her praise is a benediction. The young man's face was tight with the effort to conceal his pleasure.

"Miss Samuelson, this is Andrew Bolton."

"Miss Samuelson, I hope you'll forgive me, I just . . ."

"Why didn't you let me know you wanted to come to the theatre? Or is surprise your only weapon, Mr Bolton?" Her slight smile did not altogether take the sting out of her words.

"No. I simply wanted to visit the theatre before we met. Atmosphere, you know." I sounded defensive.

"Ha! That's the worst excuse I've heard in years."

"Actually, I didn't expect to see you here today. But now that you've arrived, could I persuade you to join me for lunch?"

"I'm not normally persuaded to do very much, Mr Bolton. Sean, do you think I can trust this man to take me to lunch? Who is he? Which character do you think he is? There are, you understand, so few characters."

Maybe, if I followed this jokey tone . . . quick . . . "Hopefully, Miss Samuelson, the kind of character with whom you'd like to have lunch?"

"Sean is smiling. So I'll say yes."

"Thank you."

"Don't thank me yet, Mr Bolton. Wait till after lunch."

I hate the invasive noise of London. Once I loved it. It constantly interrupts my conversation with you, Laura. Which I must now put aside in order to continue my work. My time with Catherine Samuelson is work. Money changes hands. I am paid to talk to people. It is perfectly honourable and certainly there is no betrayal here. We walk in silence towards a small Italian restaurant. With its gay, striped canopy and dangerously swinging sign, it is one of hundreds all over London and offers a draught of the warm south to those who are cold, even in summer.

Catherine Samuelson strode beside me in her long navy raincoat over navy sweater and cardigan and bright red skirt. She was a noticeable figure, tall and heavy, with short white-grey hair brushed off her large, pale face. In the restaurant we edged into our wooden cubicle and sat facing each other on the slightly uncomfortable benches. She did not even glance at the menu. She ordered soup, "Minestrone's fine", followed by a plate of parma ham. "Wine?" "Yes, one glass. Red, please." I followed suit. She had not been impolite but there was an abruptness in her tone that was not friendly.

"Would you object, Miss Samuelson, if I taped this conversation? It would be enormously helpful to me in preparing the programme." It's one of my few disciplines always to carry my miniature tape-recorder.

"Ah, my poor voice, trapped in that machine. I must consider my words most carefully since it will now be impossible to deny them. And we deny so much, so often. Also beware, Mr Bolton, at my age one has a tendency to lecture."

I decided not to try to charm her. I felt certain such a move would be doomed to failure. A form of attack perhaps, was best.

" 'Fundamentally, man knows nothing about himself. In order to live, he must attach a provisional meaning to himself.' I quote you, Miss Samuelson. Isn't that rather bleak?"

"You don't quote me, Mr Bolton."

"But . . ."

"No. I assure you. I was quoting Montale."

"I'm sorry." I felt a total fool, arrogant and wrong. I thought suddenly of Sarah and how she protected me from such errors on screen.

"Not at all. Don't be. I'm flattered."

"Do you believe it's true?"

"I believe it's an interesting thought. It's true for many moments of life. Very little is true all the time."

"Is there anything which is true, Miss Samuelson, all of the time?"

"All the time? Yes. As it is, so it will not be."

"Yours?" I had learned my lesson.

"Yes, to the phraseology. The thought is not original."

"So you believe everything changes?"

"And changes back again."

"Ah, our soup." I was grateful for the interruption.

We both refused the offered parmesan and were silent for a few moments, gazing down at our steamy bowls as though examining the auguries.

"I know you're scheduled to come with your team to the dress rehearsal and to the first preview. For Sam's sake I decided to be co-operative. There's a read-through tomorrow morning. Would you like to be there?"

A shock of pleasure. "Yes, very much so."

"Have you met Sam Maschlon?"

"No."

"He worked with the Berliner Ensemble for five years. This is our first production together. He's very much the commander-in-chief. Don't you think people have a positive lust for a leader – a director, president, chief-executive, whatever – someone, anyone, to tell them what to do?"

"Perhaps. But don't we also long for independence?"

"Do we? I wonder. Is it not fascinating that when the young leave the tyranny of school or the family and go straight into the tyranny of work, it's at that point they announce their independence?"

"Isn't that what you dealt with in *The Living Truth*?"

" 'Dealt with'? – I suppose that's the phrase. I've 'dealt with' the same old subjects as everyone else. Proof, perhaps, of the mythology of creativity. And I suppose I was faithful to my time. In the late '50s I was angry and political. But then *Quarto* was . . ."

"A landmark play according to . . ."

"It was nothing of the kind. I'm not modest. Were I in the first rank I wouldn't hesitate to tell you. However, I'm not. I've spent the days of my life writing for the theatre and many of my nights watching the dream begin and end. Observing the entrances and exits which I planned for the characters I created and wondering if anyone had planned my own particular journey from first line to last curtain."

"And what have you decided, Miss Samuelson?"

"That God is not a playwright."

"Perhaps He is The Director?"

"Well, Mr Bolton, certainly many directors would

agree with you! But don't misunderstand me, I'm not unproud of my life's endeavours."

"Nor should you be." God, does that sound sycophantic? How we fear that in my world. Better malice than sycophancy is the credo of my kind.

"As I grow older, I see that life and theatre are more closely linked than even I imagined. Theatre fulfils our deep longing for transformation, immortality and resurrection: we watch the actor become another; we witness the immortality of characters who have lived for thousands of years; and the nightly resurrection of the actor from the dead body of the character he has played, to take his bow – as himself.

"We've needed this dream, this metamorphosis, for over two thousand years. So little of music or painting has come to us from that time. As for the novel, it's less than four hundred years old. No, after Homer, man's first great art was practised in the theatre."

" 'All the world's a stage'?" Am I succinct or shallow?

"Indeed. Perhaps now more than ever before. Our sets become more and more elaborate. We costume ourselves in a way never before possible – and we are seduced into the thrilling belief that having created our own set and designed our own costumes, we can write our own script. Despair follows, when we find the same old story of the world, the same old parts, and the same old ending. All the world may be a stage, Mr Bolton, but there are few parts. However you transform yourself, whatever you do, wherever you go, it is, as they say about the theatre, 'plus ça change, plus c'est la même show'." She spoke the clever line and smiled. But something in me wanted to resist her.

"Can we talk about the new play . . . it's about death?"

"Not quite, Mr Bolton. You could say the subject is death, but really the subject is oblivion. I believe death is a double dealer: first, he deals us our mortal death, and then our real death – oblivion – when we are forgotten. Life to death, death to oblivion, both are short journeys, Mr Bolton. Yet we journey on, not in blissful ignorance – for this knowledge is universal – but in wilful blindness, or in childish terror, or in insane activity and accumulation of what we perceive as emblems of protection . . . Fame, 'surely if so many know me' . . . Money, 'surely if I can count me' . . . Power, 'surely, since I give orders'. Perhaps Epicurus was only half-right. Most of what we do in life may not be to try to defeat death but perhaps to defeat that dimly-glimpsed oblivion. We are, I fear, constructed for forgetfulness. The forgetfulness that we will be forgotten."

"And love? . . . Surely when we love?"

"Love is the most dangerous emotion of all for the dead. Love's the killer. Love is always the killer. The new baby, the new romance, the new wife, over time they force the dead into oblivion. Perhaps the dead are sometimes angry."

Are you angry, my darling love, my lovely Laura, that I have not spoken to you in this past hour? Are you angry? I held my hand over my eyes for a moment and I felt my mouth tighten involuntarily.

"I've offended you."

"No, no."

"A polite lie." She gazed at me. Mockingly? I must move on. I must try to keep control.

"Art — what about art? Does art defeat oblivion?"

" 'I am an artist,' the self-benediction of our time. But so few are. And of those who are, so few are great. Time alone will tell whether some unique contribution has been made, and, if the work lasts, it would have done so even if it were anonymous."

Suddenly, and with almost brutal efficiency, she snapped open her large, crocodile handbag. It had lain with a distinctly predatory air on the seat beside her, its heavy gold clasp seeming to gaze at me like some repellent, giant eye. From its mysterious depths she removed a battered envelope and a large, red notebook.

"Will you forgive me? I've just thought of some notes I meant to give Sean. My memory isn't what it was. Perhaps while I do my jottings you'd like to read the contents of this envelope. They form the genesis of the play – one a mother's letter, the other, a fragment, was written by a man. When I read them, as I often do, I am reminded of your Mr Larkin, 'Death is no different whined at than withstood'."

She gestured to the tape recorder.

"Perhaps it's unnecessary to trap the silence, Mr Bolton."

I decided to obey what was clearly a command, switched off the tape recorder and began to read.

A letter to my dead child

Child, child. Your feet. Oh, your lovely feet, your sweet feet, child. I weep constantly for them. I want to cry sweet foot, let me hold you to my face. And then sweet legs, let me stroke your legs, sweet child. Wild girl legs that used to run so fast from me, your skirt a sail around their rigging. Let me scoop your sweet body to me and rock you, child, for all the years that you will never see and that I may see, without you.

Let me place those arms of yours around me, as I bury my head upon your breast, child. Child, I think of snow, soft and white and cold. And I think of all the words men might have whispered to your breasts, that now will never be spoken. They will lie wherever all the words that were meant to be spoken lie, in some repository or lake waiting for another to speak them. But not to you. Never to you.

How many thousand kisses did I plant upon your face since the day that I first saw you, angel child? Oh, if they would sprout, your whole face would be a garden of flowers, all the flowers of spring, not summer, no full-blooded rose for you but snowdrops, anemones, a tight-budded magnolia, sprouting from your eyes and mouth, white-pink upon your cheek. On the earth which is now above you, I must plant these flowers above your barren body. What has happened to your pride-filled hair, its lustrous darkness washed by me so often, whispering words of love to your hair and kissing it over and over again, with carnal pleasure?

Hands. Have I forgotten your hands? Let me look at them again. Let me find the tiny scars — there,

*near the knuckle — childhood stigmata, rewarded by
chocolate shaped into an egg. And now it is nearly
Easter again, my Good Friday, when my love, my
own lovely child, died and not upon a cross either.
And Sunday will not bring me joy. And no Mary
Magdelene will see you walk in the garden and
mistake you for another: 'Is it you, Lord?' 'Is it
you, child?' How dare the other Mary be the only
mother whose child came back from the dead. How
can she have crucified us with her singular power
and left us all to rage that one mother brought her
child back and every other one of us condemned to
death, with death?*

*I will lament your body till the day I die, and
my rage will not die, even on the day I die. I will
never know the balm of sorrow. I will stoke my rage
beyond the grave. Eternally. And those who visit my
grave will hear me lament your feet and hands,
your limbs, your mouth and eyes and cheeks.*

*I will sing a mother's lament for her child over
and over again. The song I sang as you left . . .*

I placed the letter on the table. She glanced up at me.

"Don't ask me how I got it. It was sent to me. It's
full of wild tenderness, is it not?"

I nodded, for a moment unable to speak.

"But I'm not a tender woman. It doesn't work, the wildness of her words. Wildness cannot reach the frozen heart of loss. This excess of tender sorrow — for she is wrong, it *is* sorrow — fails. The fragment is more compelling. It is an exercise in restraint."

"Should I . . . ?"

"Yes. Read it now. I haven't finished my notes." Another order. Am I acquiring the habit of obedience?

. . . . There are certain events in life to which the only response is to fold one's hands, bow one's head and remain silent. It is not that words are inadequate. It is simply that they cannot be heard by the one to whom they are addressed. That is the first lesson. It is hard and pure. Whether you wish to learn it or not is irrelevant. You will be taught.

You may of course feel compelled to scream or perhaps being of a more gentle nature to sob. These sounds though wordless are also inadequate.

You may cease your wordless sounds early or late after the event. The timing of your silence matters not.

For some it is possible after the folding of the hands, after the bowing of the head, after the silence, or after the useless sounds, to see and to touch.

This seeing may last for hours. In some cases it may last for days. But what you see is obscured by what you cannot see. You cannot for example see a smile. You cannot see a particular movement of the head. In fact you cannot see any movement, however long you look. And they will not let you look for long. That is the second lesson. There is rarely habeas corpus beyond the grave.

You want to touch. And you can touch. But what you touch is precious to you not because of what it is but because of what it was. And was and is now signify everything. Was alive is dead.

Certain power still remains to you. The choice of clothes — vestments seems a more appropriate word — may be yours. But only if you are not of a religion which imposes certain forms of dress for death.

Having selected the clothing in which you will either burn or bury, you will be faced with decisions concerning certain rituals, to mark the reality of an event whose unreality is its prime characteristic.

Afterwards you will undertake — and now words like undertake will have an undernote — the journey home. You will open the door to a new world

*without sight or sound or touch of that lost body.
Whether you do so with grief or relief is relevant
only to you.*

*Now memory undertakes its most true function. It
has become the repository of a life. A life that is
over. And, in the vault of memory, echoes of that
life must resound, or never again be heard. It is a
heavy duty and carries with it responsibilities and
rewards.*

*And so in memory it begins: the after life after
death of the dead.*

Silently, I handed the letters back to her, and as they
disappeared with the red notebook into her bag, the
sound of the clasp as it snapped into place seemed almost
triumphant.

I spoke quickly. "My wife died a little time ago."

"How long ago?"

"Just over a year." Why, oh why, did I tell her?
What am I looking for from her?

"I will now be very cruel, Mr Bolton. Perhaps you
will not forgive me. 'My wife died' is a defining
statement. The part of Widower has certain assumed
characteristics. Just as that of Husband carries with it
guidelines for the part. There are more appropriate words

I should say to you, words which I know very well. Sadly, I also know from my own long experience that they are worthless.''

This was not what I had hoped for. Her words were not only cruel, they were facile and shallow. There was a moment's silence and a further tension between us.

''Has everyone become a character to you?'' I tried to move us onto safer ground. Does she look relieved?

''Well, don't you sometimes think it surprising, Mr Bolton, that when we say 'successful lawyer', 'famous poet', 'failed actor', 'rich businessman', 'harassed mum', further clarification seems unnecessary? Perhaps we just need to cut the cord that binds us to our childish belief that we are unique. A little humility may be all that is required.''

''So we all come from Central Casting?''

She smiled. ''Perhaps it's just the mythology of individual personality. But whoever you are — or think you are — there's no escape. There are no bribes — neither those of beauty nor talent nor wealth nor, sadly, even virtue — the river runs on.''

''Then why do you continue to write plays? You make it sound as though it's a doomed activity, and that human happiness is an impossibility.''

''Then I have failed, Mr Bolton, I've failed. And no

doubt further failure awaits me. In my new play I try to show that it is in the *acknowledgement* of the truth of our journey's end — not just death but oblivion — that happiness lies. Happiness is possible. Of that I am certain.'' Why did I feel less than reassured?

"Happiness is a decision, Mr Bolton. Make it. And don't cry." She glanced at her watch. "Good heavens, I must go. I'm so sorry, but I'll see you tomorrow, at the read-through. I'm afraid I leave you on a rather challenging note.''

"I've enjoyed it and I'm sure had we continued . . .''

"Sadly, there are no eternal conversations.''

We paid the bill and walked silently together back to the theatre. Then I left, a man in early middle-age playing the part of Widower.

EIGHT

Next morning I was nervous and excited. Signs of life, the tight stomach that rejects its normal first meal of the day, the slightly shaky hand on the blade, the muttered oath as skin is broken. Banal, universal signs of anxious anticipation.

I arrived early and stood embarrassed outside the door to the rehearsal rooms in Chelsea.

"Hi, Sam said you'd be coming. I'm Belinda the ASM – I mean Assistant Stage Manager."

"Hello, Belinda. Actually, I acted at college, so I do remember what ASM stands for."

"Good. 'Cos sometimes, I tell you, I don't. Anyway," she opened the heavy, wooden door and we entered the high-ceilinged hall, its floor stencilled with chalk markings, "follow me into my little cubby-hole at the back. We can have a coffee before the egos arrive." She handed me a plastic cup of steaming black liquid, opened a carton of milk and deluged the coffee in a flood of white, making it simultaneously aesthetically unpleasing and cold.

"Thanks. That's great," I lied, as we edged out of the accurately described cubby-hole.

"Mr Bolton. You're here before us. Such dedication! Let me introduce you to Sam. Sam's that elegant leather-jacketed, red-haired giant coming through the doorway."

'Now, why can't I always be introduced like that, Catherine? Hello. Catherine told me *she*'d invited you." He smiled. "Just teasing. I'm pleased you've come. You can make it clear that I'm the real driving force round here and Catherine just writes what I tell her. Morning, darling."

He kissed the top of her head and even ruffled her hair a bit.

"That's enough, Sam. We'll shock Mr Bolton."

I wished she'd stop calling me Mr Bolton. But it was not my place to invite her friendship and she certainly hadn't said "Call me Catherine".

"Miss Samuelson, have a coffee."

"Thank you, Belinda. *Without* the milk, Belinda."

As the actors arrived, "Morning everyone. If I break down at an inappropriate moment . . . my cat's just died" . . . "God, it's gloomy in here" . . . "Morning

Sam, I like the leather jacket'', I sensed their slight uneasiness at my presence. Sam rescued me.

"You all know Andrew Bolton and about his programme on Catherine and the play. This morning he's going to sit in on a reading. No filming or notes, nothing until the dress rehearsal, that's right, Andrew?''

"Yes, absolutely. I really appreciate . . .'

'Mr Bolton, come and sit here beside me.'' Catherine Samuelson motioned to me and I self-consciously joined her at a large table which faced an area marked out in white chalk. The actors walked, script in hand, into various positions. Sam – the 'red-haired giant' – stood in front of them, his back to the table, and started to speak rather formally and gravely. He was very much the Director performing his script.

"In life we choose words almost automatically from some script in our head. How did we learn the lines? How did we absorb the tone, the right vocal note for 'I love you', 'I'm sorry', 'Don't go'? We learned it through observation of others, through stories, films, theatre; and having learned that note we then learned to strike it in deceit, in anger, in despair. In deceit we're all actors – it comes naturally. And now you – professional actors – must look for truth in this grand deceit – a play, this play.

"There are many ways into a play – through the door

of character, through the door of historical setting, through the door of political resonance. I always start with the Word." He opened the script. "Look at it. Any word. It lies inert on the page. It's tired. It's been on a journey, perhaps a perilous journey, during which it did battle with other words – a battle to the death. Now victorious, but exhausted, it takes its rightful place within the hierarchical structure of the sentence, the sentence which knows its place in the order of the paragraph, and now it must wait and wonder: 'Will I be read? Or will I be spoken? Will the echo of the sound I make reverberate again?'

"Ladies and gentlemen, you are speakers of the Word. Yours is the art of generosity and surrender. You slip the chains of self and slide into otherness. The integrity of personality is under assault each time your surrender is witnessed. That is why your art is little understood and sometimes feared. Remember, actors were once thought blasphemous because they presumed to do the work of God in creating new persons. You transform yourselves; sometimes you become the dead and are then resurrected. Have you noticed the extra intensity of the applause given to the resurrected actor when after his dramatic death he steps forward to take his bow?" Everyone laughed. He smiled, almost shyly. "Today I won't interrupt. I'll listen as you search for, and

I hope find, the hidden rhythm of the words. Let's begin.''

"CAN YOU HEAR ME AT THE BACK? I REPEAT. CAN YOU HEAR ME AT THE BACK? AT THE BACK OF YOUR MIND? PICK A VOICE, FOR ME, FROM THE ECHO CHAMBER. FROM THE 'AUDITORY IMAGINATION'. WELL, GET IN THERE. ROOT AROUND. GET ME A VOICE. NO. NOT THAT ONE. BE QUIET FOR A MOMENT AND LISTEN. YES, THAT'S IT. THAT'S THE VOICE. THANK YOU. THANK YOU. AND NOW, CAN YOU HEAR ME IN 'THE DEEP HEART'S CORE'? CAN I GO THERE? PLEASE. WILL YOU LET ME? Mother used to say, 'One must never beg'. So here are my orders. PAY ATTENTION. STOP! STOP NOW. Whatever is in your mind, KILL IT. Whatever story, dream, worry, row, KILL IT. KILL IT NOW. Whoever lurks there from past or present, BANISH THEM. I'm greedy for your soul. I want to plant a story there. And then another . . . But first, I must MURDER your voices. The ones in your head. OK. All gone? Wasn't that painless? Only mine now? Certain?

THANK YOU. Thank you for your mind tonight. Good evening, ladies and gentlemen.

May I introduce myself? My name is . . . Oh, it doesn't matter. Names rarely matter. My mother, when she was dying, called everyone by the same name. 'Makes no difference,' she said. The name she called everyone? George, actually, which was not the name of her son or of her husband. What was she like? Here's a quick memory, a memory of Mother. She was forever putting on lipstick, then blotting it off, whispering 'Stain, I want stain.' Looking back, I suppose she was always dressed for a funeral. Depressive? Oh dear, no. If anything, she was a manic oppressive.

My father? God, you're an inquisitive lot. My father lived on hate and money. And the more he hated, the more money he made, and the more money he made, the more he hated. There is, as you know ladies and gentlemen, no more dispiriting view than the view from the top.

What did you say? Did someone comment on my accent? My accent doesn't match the suit? You're so right. I knew you'd notice. I just knew you were snobs. Would you listen more atten-tively if they matched, the appearance and the voice? Shall I come on again, with a different voice? It's not a problem. Like you, I can give any performance.

Tonight my performance is, I suppose, that of Maître d' – Maître Death in a way. I am the Master who will give life to the dead. To certain 'chosen ones' from this well-filled graveyard. I will allow them to tell their tale, to have their little ego trip. But I'll keep it short, darlings. I promise. SHUSH. Can't you hear them, rustling in the wings, fluttering round the actors, their conduits to the living? God, they're so **desperate** to speak. Desperate to be remembered, even for minutes. I love to torture them, make them wait. I am what I made myself – which is The Master, here.

Let me ask you, how did you make yourself? Who helped you? Come on, be truthful, was it the living or the dead? A chorus of both perhaps? Did you ever say thank you? For the you you are, or think you are. I know it's difficult. Being who you are just doesn't come naturally, does it? You have to fight against all those millions of people vomited into the world, all looking for SELF. Like this little group I'm going to introduce you to. Later, when **I'm** ready.

First, a declaration of responsibility. These characters you are about to see and listen to, are mine. Of course, I don't actually own them. After all, one doesn't own one's children, but I did create them. I could have put them in anything, but I decided to, well, play with them, if you follow my meaning.

OK, OK, I accept Catherine Samuelson may be the author of the play, in real life. But you haven't come here for real life have you? My God, you get enough of that at home, eh? Yes, madam, I bet you do. Real life. Lovely turn of phrase, don't you think? What is life? Ah, ladies and gentlemen, what a question! Life is grammar, darlings. I am. I was. I will not be. Repeat after me.

I am.

I was.

I will not be.

Tense is all. That's all.

The title of the play? It's Catherine Samuelson's. *The Book*. Yes, I know it's confusing. She doesn't trust simplicity. Evidently some poet called Mallarmé was long thought to be writing a masterpiece called 'The Book' which was never published.

Catherine Samuelson was, for some reason, inspired by this, and called her play *The Book*. Get it? Neither do I. There is another interpretation, of course, but I won't bore you . . .

Anyway, real people, flesh and blood people, over the next two hours – yes, sir, it's that long, only one interval – will persuade you they are not themselves. Actors have always done that but I still feel you need to be reminded. Though you're all familiar with the technique of not being yourself. Such a relief, isn't it?

Lies are going to be told. I thought it only fair to warn you.

Forget your programme. Who reads them anyway. There's a long piece by Catherine Samuelson, so-called creator of the play. Famous for her reticence about her suffering in the concentration camps. 'There is enough evil in your own time, if you wish to comment.' Oh, I do like that, darlings, don't you? Positively blazes with integrity. Her essay in the programme is downright self-serving. If you ask me, she just wants to bring to your attention what a C-O-M-P-L-E-X human being she is.

But me – I'm keeping it simple. I don't want

any convoluted, contrived stuff here. I want it to be the way it used to be. A man just telling his story. Voices entering the mind. So it's just my characters, telling their little histories, 'leurs petites histoires', I love that line.

LIFE'S A MONOLOUGE, DON'T YOU THINK? Everyone crying out, 'MY STORY, LISTEN TO MY STORY.' But we've heard it before, angel. Did you know there are only four temperaments, melancholic, choleric, phlegmatic, sanguine? Desperate to place yourself? We long for individuality, and we long to be a part of a group, any group. Bit of a contradiction, for INDIVIDUAL YOU, don't you think?

Now, who's going to bring all this to life, you ask? Fascinating question. A cast, sweetie. People like you. CAST CALL! CAST CALL! DON'T GET UP, LADIES AND GENTLEMEN. I'M NOT CALLING YOU. STAY SEATED. THIS IS NOT YOUR PERFORMANCE.

Some of the cast are Stanislavsky slaves. Let me quote the late great Konstantin. 'Our type of creativeness is the CONCEPTION and BIRTH of a new being.' Think about it, ladies and gentlemen. About the part your parents wrote for you before you were born. Pleased with the script, were you? Bully for you.

Oh, they're becoming impossibly restless in the wings – sobbing and sighing and stamping their feet.

So here, tripping on, and about to 'give birth', Philippa Sturridge, who will BE ANNABELLE HAWKSLEY.

Imogen Caine, we call her Imo, will bring forth KATE FENTON, horribly. Which is perfect for the role.

Tony Worth, who's worth anyone's money, will become PETER BISHOP.

Charles Pinden 'plays' THEO BISHOP, I use the word advisedly. He is unhappy in the part. Who wouldn't be?

Desmond Hennessy will speak to you in the voice of MICHAEL O'HALLORAN. The accent's authentic. You last saw him in *Hamlet*? Let me ask you, did he see your after-supper performance that night? Remember the lies you told about your father? And no ghost came to punish you.

Here's Angela Evans – OUR LADY OF LUST. Perfect casting, as you can see. God, just look at that body. Yes, she went to RADA, darlings, but she also w-o-r-k-s o-u-t. Forgive me, ladies and gentlemen, but 'a man's a man for a' that'. Her hair? What is this — Ode To a Haircut?

Oh dear, all these names. Names of the actors, names of the characters. Would you be You with another name? 'A Rose by any other name' . . . could be called Sarah. SORRY! Always loved the name Rose and rosy little Sarahs. Anyway, think of all those lucky bastards, whose names have lasted and will outlast us all, Lear, Hamlet, Othello, and the daddy of them all, Oedipus. He's had a long life. Sometimes I think I can hear him, tragic Oedipus, crying, 'I am Oedipus and my mother loved me. She longed for me, I tell you. I, Oedipus, lay down with my mother.' Ladies and gentlemen, you know I can almost hear him scream, 'Mother, Mother,' in his ecstasy. Oh yes, darling. I think he knew all along. That's the lie — of the lay. Makes me shiver to think of it. Pleasure? Don't pin that on me. Think of the consequences!

Mother was wrong. Name IS the name of the game. Too sexist, am I with all this talk of men? Electra, Phaedra, Juliet, there's a list for you. And Medea, played by a man, first time around.

Oh yes. Surprised? But the great emotions are genderless. Let me ask you, is ecstasy masculine or feminine? What gender is grief? Medea's not a monster, she's like all mothers, darling. They all kill their children, one way or another. It's the same old story, from Oedipus to Hamlet, cherchez la mère.

Finally, please remember what I said earlier – THEY'RE ALL DEAD. The characters, I mean, silly, not the actors. Gawd, where-do-you-come-from? The actors are giving life to the dead. Just like you do, darling, when you play your part, which has been much played before. Anyway, just remember, before you get too uppity, once upon a time, they were, as you are now, alive. And now they are dead. AND LADIES AND GENTLEMEN, IT'S A FACT, UNIVERSALLY ACKNOWLEDGED, THAT A DEAD BODY IS IN NEED OF DISPOSAL.

Now, let me deal with this as tastelessly as possible. Let me give you some facts, darlings, about the most popular modern method – referred to as cremation. Actually it's a very old method – goes back to the Vikings. It's been out of fashion for ages but now back again. Burial has become S-O P-A-S-S-É.

In simple language, cremation is the burning of your body and the crushing of your bone, in order that what remains will fit into the smallest possible container. Crème-brûlée, you might say. But without the sugar. Neatness is all, darlings.

I'll go through this as quickly as possible. First, we need for the sake of your nearest and dearest to stop you smelling to high heaven and making all those who in their various ways loved your body, violently sick. Just think of the ways your body's been loved. Well, it's NOT SO LOVABLE NOW. So, we inject a solution to stop the smell. A sort of eternal deodorant. Then, and I hate to be crude, however orifices must be stuffed, and not in the way you remember, angel.

Since you now look ghastly, so pale, waxy actually, we have to dolly you up so as not to frighten the – well – the living, the ones 'not yet called', so to speak. You know, most people don't look frightened when they die. They look trusting, actually, at the end of now, their now. Same old trust. Same old betrayal.

When you've been 'done over' at the funeral parlour, they'll slip you into a coffin, though not of the quality used in burial. Actually, it's a cheap wooden coffin, burns more easily. And there you'll be for a day or so, depending on your religion, what your god said, on the subject of how and when they should dispose of your body. I'm afraid you're going to be handled by strangers, darling. Sorry about that.

When you arrive at the crematorium, they'll whizz you into a kind of utility room and onto a trolley.

Then, the service. Please remember they're very, very busy little bees at the crematorium. So the service is a maximum of twenty minutes, angel. Take a tip from me. If you can afford it, book double time. Less rushed. However rushed you were in life, darling, one does hope for a little dignity now. For old times' sake.

Then, with everybody weeping copiously, or dignified in pain not boredom, you hope – you will disappear behind heavy dark curtains. Oh, the drama of it! However, this is not when the deed is done, darlings, oh no.

Later, could be much later, they will burn you. And it will take up to one and half hours to reduce you, flesh and dear old bone, hair and gristle, to dust, which is, I'm afraid, mixed up with what remains of the coffin. NOTHING'S PURE YOU, DARLING, even in death. And then you need to cool down. Which takes time. But you're no longer impatient.

After that, some nice man with a metal detector will remove any bits of metal hanging around. Yes, that old pace-maker, and oh, ladies, I'm SO SORRY to tell you this, SILICONE is GHASTLY, my darlings. You would be D-I-S-G-U-S-T-E-D at how it burns.

When you've finally cooled down, you're sucked into a little hoover-like bag, darling, and back into Utility. Then a quick magimix for the bones and you're ground into dust, dark grey, 'dust thou art, and into dust shalt thou return'. How right they were. Then, into a little plastic jar, to await your final resting place. Under a rose tree probably, which will bear your name. But, and this is important, usually on a rental basis only, for five to eight years. It's AMAZING how many people don't continue the rental. Yes, honestly, I know it's shocking. OF COURSE, IT WON'T HAPPEN TO YOU. MY GOD, THEY LOVE YOU SO MUCH. THEY'LL NEVER FORGET YOU.

And now finally,

'The fire and the rose are one –
In the cre-ma-tor-ium!'

Did you know that eighty per cent of people in
England now choose this method of disposal? It's a
growing market. Invest, darlings, invest. Only four-
teen per cent in France did you say? Really! Perhaps
French women, after all those years of 'le maquill-
age', wouldn't allow themselves to be burned. Not
beyond their capability to seduce the worm, I
suppose? And the men? Well, cherchez la femme,
chéri – comme normale! Tonight, however, we're
staying in an old-fashioned graveyard. Hence the set.
Tomorrow night, who knows?

Yes, sir, I heard your question, 'TELL US ABOUT
THE SET?' Stand up. Oh, shy, are we? Well, what's
your set like – the set on which you play your part?
You, AT THE BACK, I know it was you – let me ask
you, if someone lived in Venice all their lives, are
they likely to be a better person? Is there any
evidence? Does the set, the Venetian set, make a
difference? Does your set influence you, at home, or
in the office?

You know, I often wonder, did moving inside, into
theatres, do damage? All those hundreds of years,
competing with the bird song and the clouds, the

trees, the colours. What competition! Then a few hundred years ago, we got cold feet, so to speak.

Well, this set is movable, bits of marble, stone, earth, Alistair Crowden in his minimalist period. The red silk cross waving about at the back? We know death is ecumenical, but Sean thought we should still use the symbol of the Cross. I hope those of you who are non-Christian amongst us, NO, DON'T PUT UP YOUR HANDS, those of you will be . . . Christian, in your attitude. I think the Cross is very evocative. It was designed by Alistair Crowden's good friend, Sean Cates. Outing? What are you talking about? We're full of gay pride here, sir.

With regard to sets, read Catherine Samuelson on Aristotle's key points about the real unreality of the theatre. Know what? Think of it as the real unreality of life. Real chairs, real houses, real trees, but what is a real person? Hamlet's more real to the world than you are, dearie.

Are we all doomed to play a role that's often been played before? Don't you ever feel trapped between the hordes of the dead and the yet to be born, all of them, knocking on the door? Not to mention the millions here now – INDIVIDUAL YOU VERSUS MASS

THEM — it's an eternal tension, darlings. But enough about YOU.

Let's talk about ME. Who's playing me? Let's call him Max. Yes. I could be adequately played by a man called Max. Now, let me take off my mask. And underneath — VOILA — as you can see, take my word for it, Max's mask. My face? You think you could tell something from my face? Will it talk to you? No, sweetie, it will tell nothing. 'Can I infer my spirit from my physiognomy?' Can you? No I'm afraid you can't. So, get yourself a mask and stick with it. Get used to it and, most importantly, make sure it fits.

AND TONIGHT, LADIES AND GENTLEMEN, we've got some delicious agony for you, the agony of others. The kind you prefer. And, sweet ladies, kind gentlemen, voyeurs, 'mon semblable, mon frère', or perhaps 'ma soeur', the agony of others makes voyeurs of us all. Of course, it's vitally important to us to believe we are before an audience of REAL PEOPLE. I mean the whole thing is based on this presumption. ARE YOU REAL OUT THERE? Oh, I do hope so.

I'm The Master but I'm also your guide, your humble guide, ladies and gentlemen, round this particular graveyard. Though, as you can hear, I ain't no Virgil, and we're not going round in Circles here.

We all of us hope there's a Master of Ceremonies, don't we? God, perhaps? Well, He seems to be as silent here as He was on earth. Can't get a word out of Him. Perhaps His silence is eternal. But like you, all of us up here need the illusion that SOMEONE must be watching. Even when no one is. We're all doomed to be eternally alone. Remember, if you die first, they don't bury you with your mother. Even mothers don't give up life just to be with you. No matter how often they called you 'darling, sweetie pie.' Mostly they hang on. Mama doesn't answer the last 'Mama, Mama.'

Oh dear, I'd better get off, hadn't I? Anyone left I haven't offended? Any widowers in the house? Anyone lost a child? I suppose you know that 'after the first death there is no other'? Good. Oh God, I'm tired. AND NOW LADIES AND GENTLEMEN, SWEET LADIES, KIND GENTLEMEN, DREAM. DREAM OF MICHAEL, 'who was once handsome and tall as you'. Look at him now, handsome and tall and, well, dead. He's got his pathetic little story to tell. He's looking for remembrance. He hasn't a chance. Unless, of course, you give him houseroom in your mind. Got room in your mind for Michael? Little shit that he is, and was. He doesn't like facing the audience, so I said to him, 'OK, Michael, turn your back.' Have you ever seen them face anyone? Or listen to anyone? They only listen to themselves, to their own clamour.

GO ON, MICHAEL, tell your filthy little story. He's in a panic. They're beginning to forget him. Even his mother can't remember certain things about him – yes, even his mother. So he needs you to listen – 'cos he's fading fast. Silence everyone. Listen to Michael. Michael with his back to you – telling the history of his story.''

"I didn't waste my life. I found my cause. And I killed for it. Not often, you know. Three people. To be fair, an accident took two of them. So, I don't feel completely responsible. No one ever found out it was me. No one ever questioned me. Sometimes the fact that I did it just – well, it just slipped my mind.

I didn't know the man I shot. I did what I was told. You could say I was good at my job, because I never got caught. Though, getting caught is not actually a failure, you know. I don't see that as a failure. Not at all. Some of the things I remember didn't happen, but should have. The funerals happened. I know that. I always noted the date. And I'd think, 'My God, did I do that?' I'm kind of mystified by the mystery of it, if you know what I mean.

They told me I was an idealist. Others called me a terrorist. Some said I was a paramilitary. But when it came down to it, I existed to kill. I know the reasons. I don't need to hear them again, or to tell them again. Let it stand. I killed. Once someone said to me 'Isn't it better than working at the Co-op?' Which I thought was a foul thing to say. I'm trying to make myself as attractive as I can in the hope you'll remember me.

Now I'm dead. From cancer – of the blood. There was something wrong with my blood; you could say I had bad blood. It was a real surprise, I can tell you. I mean that's what I felt. Surprised. I thought I'd go some other way. I wasn't afraid to meet My Maker. Oh no, towards the end I was only afraid of where I'd be buried. I remember the girl, Alice O'Reilly, in the pair who were blown up, accidentally. Well, she lost her stomach. I mean, there was nothing there. At night, I dreamed she was . . . how can I say this . . . swelling over me. Trying to make me into a baby. Yes, trying to make me into a baby, in her stomach. To make up to her for losing it, her stomach, and her womb. God, I hate that word, womb. It gives me the creeps. I felt I'd never get out of her stomach. I'd be trapped there. And I'd wake screaming. So, when I knew I wasn't going to get out of this dying thing, I asked my mother not to bury me close to Alice O'Reilly. She looked at me, hard and said, 'And why not? What did you have to do with Alice O'Reilly?' 'Nothin',' I said. And Alice O'Reilly's mother met my mother and me in the street. And she was full of obscenities, about what she'd do to the lad that did it. It was disgusting. I can't tell you all the things she said. My mother started to cry, but Alice O'Reilly's mother kept on whispering in a hoarse voice . . . 'I'd eat the ones who devoured my girl, my Alice. Eat them, and excrete them. I'd eat them and excrete them. I'd eat . . .'

I was sick, I can tell you, to hear a mother speak like that, a woman, for God's sake. And a mother. God, I'll tell you something, I'm glad I'll never meet another mother, ever. They can crucify you, because it's mothers who brought us into the world.

I used to love the girls I was with. They could walk, oh, you know, hips swinging, so full of themselves, that they'd leave you faint. And with them there were other, different explosions and whispers and screams. But then I'd remember the thing I did. And I'd be sick. Yes, flesh makes a sound when it . . . Then nothing. Anyway, back to mothers. To tell the truth, Jesus, I really admire them, even though they terrify me. Because they know, or at least they can guess, what it took to make a human body.

And it wouldn't leave me – this idea of not being

buried in Ireland. And I wouldn't let anyone pretend I wasn't dying. I wasn't going to be treated like a fool. I begged my mother to take me to England, to bury me there. 'No one in our family's ever been buried there.' 'Well, I want to be. And my Da works there.' They've been separated for years. He used to beat her. But you know something, I liked him. I really liked him. Anyway, she was a difficult woman. 'It can't be so hard. Arrange this for me, Ma. Please, just this. Take me to England. I can stay with my Da and then you can visit.'

I asked her every day and every day, for months, she said no. I told her finally, that I'd find my own way not to be buried in that churchyard. And I did. I wasn't going to be swallowed up by Alice O'Reilly, in the grave. She wanted me. I knew that. 'I'm off,' I said to my mother, when I was in remission, which sounded like a religious retreat. I'm off in more ways than one, you might say. I was nothing. I know that. I'm not a fool. But I'll be remembered. You'll remember me, won't you?

Don't be too hard on me. Think of all the other ways they could have died. I mean, anything could have happened to them. She could have died in a car crash, or got sick herself. And it's for sure something would have happened to her, some time. That's for certain. I suppose you could say they were all going to die anyway. I only rearranged the time. There's something like God about that, don't you think? That's what I think, anyway. And like I said, I always went to church on the day they were buried. My church. As a mark of respect, you could say.

I'm not a coward. No one could call me a coward. I didn't waste my life. I've no regrets. None at all. If you think what you're doing is right, then why feel guilty? Anyway, that's what I tell myself. I was only frightened, not guilty. I was frightened all right – of Alice O'Reilly. Who, I kept thinking, would come to get me. And swallow me. She was very thin. I kept thinking of that.

It's not madness, you know. I'm not mad. Life and Death – what is it? Good dreams and bad dreams. But it's all dreams. And mine is over now. I'm here, buried in England, as I wanted. But I'm amongst strangers. Can't be helped.

Max asked me – he's like a commander here – what do you remember? They're very keen on memory in this place. Our own treasure chest of memory, you see.

'What's your clearest memory of an element? Is it air, water, fire or earth?' he asked me, on my first day here.

'I remember air,' I said. 'What I remember most is air. Fighting for it once. No. That's not true. What I remember is water . . .'

And the girl, Annabelle, who I lie beside, water is what

she remembers most. And to have to share this memory with someone like me – you have to tell the truth, nothing else is possible here – well, it makes water filthy for her. She feels she must wash her memory clean. And I'm sad for that. I like her. And she's not Alice O'Reilly. To lie close to her is not so difficult. Let's put it this way, I've known worse girls to lie beside. And honest to God, I don't remember sex at all. Isn't that amazing? I was, as I used to say to my brother, mad for it.

'You're mad for it, and mad without it, and only sane for a few minutes after you get it. Face it, fella – you're mad anyway,' he'd say to me. I miss him. I miss my brother.

Max said once that I was evil, but it was a careless evil. That I only half saw things. And even the things I saw, I didn't understand. So I just carelessly mowed down life, like a machine out of control.

'Max,' I said, 'there was nothing careless about it. I planned it, sometimes the plans went wrong.'

"You'll know what I mean in time, Michael. Believe me, you'll become silent."

"Like the grave? And in it. Isn't that good, Max?"

"Good?"

"Good. Yes. You know, funny?

So that's my story. I'm sick of it now. I've told it so often. Max, help me, Max. They're beginning to forget. No one will help me, now that they know what I am. MAX, MAX, PLEASE."

"Oh, all right then, Michael. I'll ask them. Go and sit over there, by the stones. I'll do my best for you. IS THERE A LIFE IN THE HOUSE FOR MICHAEL? Is there a vacant life? No! Nothing's available for Michael then. And he's desperate not to be forgotten. Go on, be generous. Surely there's a face or body he could move into. Ah, well, I thought not. All too attached to your own . . . for now.

AND NOW, LADIES AND GENTLEMEN, it's the turn of Annabelle, our clever little ingénue. You know the kind I mean. Every three years there's a new lot pouring out of universities, brainy and beautiful. Sadly, she's a dead ingénue. The 'jeunesse dorée' is a bit lacklustre, if you'll forgive me. She doesn't like it one little bit here. It's tantrum time, with our little girl who had everything. Proper little madam. You may start, Annabelle. **Miss Annabelle, you may start**."

"Max, I want to laugh. Should I laugh at the beginning? I always laughed a lot."

"In life?"

"Yes, in life."

"But you're dead now, Annabelle."

"But, I'm trying to catch how I was, when I lived."

"Yes. But it's after you're dead, Annabelle. Try to remember that — all the time. It's after you're dead."

"It's difficult, Max."

"Oh, come on, Annabelle. It's a chance to be remembered, for a moment. By this group, anyway."

"Shall I start? And, Max, I don't feel comfortable speaking about the love part."

"All right, angel. Now come on, they're waiting, the audience is waiting, madam. MICHAEL! Stop sulking, or I'll ask you to leave the stage."

"Max, why are you more interested in her life than

mine? You've always cared more about her than me, haven't you?''

"Shut up, Michael, you've had your turn. GET OUT OF THE WAY. SO SORRY FOR THE INTERRUPTION, ANNABELLE. GO ON, DARLING.''

"My name is Annabelle. My name was Annabelle. I will begin at the end, since, unlike you, I know it. Mine is a shorter story than most, so I won't keep you long. You have so little time. Don't look so surprised. Time's running out for you, not me.

Well then, are we ready? Let us begin. Let's begin in the old-fashioned way. Once upon a time, I was, as you are now, alive. I was a beloved, only child, and a worshipped girl. I was worshipped, literally worshipped, by a boy. I do not exaggerate. I did not misunderstand. Are you profoundly loved? I remember, they said it's all that matters. Do you believe it's all that matters? 'In the end,' they always said that, 'in the end, it's all that matters.' When you get down to it, do they still say that? Wasn't there a song? 'Love is all you need.' And I remember a line: 'What will survive of us is love.'

Do you believe that? What will remain of you is love? And is it the love you got? Or the love you gave? In the end, I didn't care about love, to be honest. And honestly now, you must trust me, if I'm going to tell you a lie, I'll warn you. Some lies are true. Some, so wonderful, it seems an absolute shame to pretend they're only the truth, 'I love you to death', *par exemple*. I spent six months in Paris and will occasionally introduce *en passant*, God, this makes me laugh, a few words in French. I do it to remind me of the taste of the language. Don't you think language tastes? No? I do. Anyway, why don't I begin at the end? It's all you're certain of. Honest Injun, as my brother used to say. Did I say I was an only child? Well, I lied. So, as my brother used to say, 'Honest Injun'. His name? George, actually.

True lies are essential to us all. And they're mostly about love, actually. Sorry about the actually, but that's the way I talk. Now, you expected me to say, used to talk. But I talk still, here and there. Think about it.

Mostly, my mother hears me. But I don't tell her everything. You know what mothers are. They know everything anyway. They just don't want you to tell them. But you probably knew that already.

And I talk to him, my old lover. Someday he won't need to hear the echo. Maybe, she, when she comes, will want to silence me. Well, there's no maybe about that. But I digress. Once upon a time, I was, as you are now, alive. Do you know you're alive? I mean, really know it?

Do you believe you will die? Do you believe you'll be forgotten? Really believe it? Well, I don't blame you. Neither did I. Let me give you a certainty. In an uncertain world, as they say, the only thing of which you can be certain is that you're going to die and be forgotten. So what? So everything. Start there. Work back. I know what I'm talking about.

I'm the daughter of Anne and Duncan Hawksley, who live in the very pretty village of Dunsfield, within commuting distance of London. There, my father is a very senior civil servant in Her Majesty's Government. He was knighted in the year of my death, which was, I suppose, a 'consolation'. He is a superior person. Do you know the rhyme?

> 'My name is George Nathanial Curzon,
> I am a most superior person.
> My cheeks are pink,
> My hair is sleek,
> I dine at Blenheim twice a week.'

Well, we had our own version:

> 'My name is Duncan Gallowshiel Hawksley,
> Government ministers like to talk to me,
> My plans superior
> Charm my inferior

Who goes on TV to repeat them *precisely*.'

Yes, he's a most superior person, well, intellect, a most superior intellect. My mother is Anne Hawksley, Lady Hawksley, and she is in mourning for me who was – tenses really matter here – her daughter. My mother, I think, but you can never be certain about love, loved me more than she loved George, my brother. My bothersome brother. Broken arms, yes both of them, broken leg, skis as if it was life itself. And so far, to everyone's astonishment, has not yet discovered death. But he's trying. Death, just isn't interested yet. No. Death was interested in me. Clever old me. And I was such a clever girl. I got my degree. Unlike George, who was sent down. He was involved in a drug scandal, a very serious scandal. No. I won't tell you about it. This is my story, not George's. He'll get his own chance one day. And I got a job, straight from university. Clever, clever old me. George spent a year going round the world. Got home 'just in time' as they say. He caught me – on my way out. As the others did, as my lover did. 'He doesn't know what to do with himself, that man. He's besotted with you.' My mother used to say that. Are you loved like that? Besottedly? I loved him too. It was impossible not to. I had no choice, which in a way is a pity. 'The man desires the woman. And the woman desires the man's desire.' I read that in a book someone brought to the hospital and I thought, that's a good, true lie. It's a lie which could have lasted well into my future. Yes, oh yes, once upon a time, I had a future. With a hey diddle diddle . . .

But my future became a kind of dream of the past for others. A dream, in which I stayed 'alive', for quite some time after I died. People could feel my presence, you know. I guided them. They talked to me and I told them what to do. Go on, ask them. They'll tell you. It goes like this, their litany. 'It was late at night, my God, I was frightened and I just . . . sort of felt her there with me. And I said, Come on, come on — Annabelle, tell me which turning. Come on girl, I'm lost. Christ, I was frightened, but she did . . . She showed me the way.' That was George — lost again.

They see me, oh yes. They turn corners and 'I swear to God I saw her. She was walking — and the hair — you know, the hair was all loose. She had beautiful hair. Beautiful.' My mother, of course.

'And there she was. I reached out and touched her, and . . . and.' And nothing. That's the truth. Only from him. We have a sort of communion. It fades, of course, when they start to forget us. And, of course, eventually they do. Eventually, everyone does. We all know that here, the forgotten and the about-to-be forgotten. After you're forgotten – oblivion, eternal oblivion. I don't want to think about it. It's not going to happen for a while . . .

No one reaches out to touch me now. They burden me with flowers and weight me down with marble. Terrified, I suppose, that I might get up. They don't take many chances do they, the living? If they don't lock you into wood and bolt it down and then, just to be certain, pile earth on top of you, then a cement or marble surround and possibly a few urns, if they don't do that, they burn you, for God's sake. They burn you. Sometimes, you've asked for it. Environmentally conscious, in your conscious days of conscious physical life, when you just knew, it really, finally, couldn't happen, that your painted toenails and your toned and tautened body and your creamy skin – 'sun's so bad for it' – would burn. Not lightly tanned, no, I'm talking real burns here. Your own precious body is not going to be ashes. You didn't really mean it. Did you know that babies leave no ashes? Maybe it's best.

Though I was lightly tanned when I left I didn't burn. They laid me to rest . . . It was early summer. Date? You want the date? Why?

I died young. And if you're young it's the usual list:

motor cycle crash — 'why, oh why did we buy it for him?'

car crash — 'oh God no, it can't be true. But we warned him over and over again . . . '

cancer, cervix — 'huge survival rate . . . mostly'

suicide — 'God, he was such a beautiful boy, hanged himself'

drugs — 'he was always wild'

fell through a roof — 'trying to save his bloody cat'

drowned — 'trying to save her bloody dog'

ran across the road — 'straight in front of a car — driver was distraught — just distraught, spent a year in therapy'

and don't forget meningitis — 'running around in the morning, dead that same night. Only daughter. Mother hysterical'

and polio — 'it's coming back, like TB they say'.

Now there's AIDS. Max calls it the 'new quick-step in the age-old dance of Eros and Thanatos'.

You see, old deaths, new deaths, they're nothing.

How did I die? Why do you want to know? Curiosity? I'm dead, that's all that counts, to me. Oh God, I'm crying. I must stop. They don't like that here.

Max is telling me to leave the stage. All right, Max, I'll go. I've no fight left. But please, Max, after I exit, please dim the lights. Just for a moment, Max, P-L-E-A-S-E. Let them remember, once upon a time, I was, as they are now, alive. P-L-E-A-S-E, MAX.''

"Don't cry, Annabelle. Don't cry. She's a bit hoity-toity but I'm really fond of that girl. Lights. Goodbye, goodbye Annabelle. Wasn't that S-A-D! And she was perfectly cast. Annabelle loved life. It's not reciprocated. People are always making that mistake. No one warned Annabelle it was going to be such a short run. Nobody told her. But honestly, it happens every day to some Annabelle, somewhere. And they all take it so personally . . .''

"EXCUSE ME. I'VE DECIDED TO SPEAK.''

"MAJOR? MY GOD — I WASN'T EXPECTING THIS!''

"Don't call me that. My name is Alistair Dunning — writer. And I don't want your smart-arse introduction either. I know what I want to say and it will take precisely four and a quarter minutes. I think it better if I address them from here. What's your name? Max, isn't it? Would you care to move . . ."

"Why, of course, Major, of course."

"This is not a confession. It's a statement.

I was on the left of the boy as he fell. He didn't look surprised. I always read in stories of these events, 'he looked surprised as he fell,' but for him it wasn't true. Though I told his mother so. It seemed the right thing to do.

No, as he fell he looked, as indeed he was . . . unfinished. And 'unfinished' was what he whispered to me as I, fearful and ashamed of my fear, bent over one of the many who fell that day – and many-a-one fell that day. And all of them were more individual before, than after, the bullet or the grenade, and able to explain the subtle this-or-that which made them definitively one, before they became one of the many of the many-a-one who fell that day.

His hand fluttered the way they say a girl's hand flutters, though, truth to tell, no girl's hand has ever fluttered over me. I don't know why. And then his long, young hand seemed to jump and jerk above his chest and

weakly beat against his breast pocket, gurgling 'Unfi-
ni . . . .' I put my hand on top of his to steady what he
could no longer bend to his will – the fingers which had
held the pen which had dug some furrow with words in
an ancient pattern and were now about to cease their
digging. I opened his pocket and found the white paper
on which blood had mixed with ink to make a kind of
patriotic hieroglyphic in red, white and blue. 'Unfinished.'
He finished the word this time.

I looked down at him as he died and tried to lie to
him with my eyes. I knew he couldn't hear but I tried to
make my eyes imply, 'Yes, yes. I will.' His body, puppet-
like, seemed for a minute electrified in a frantic fit, a
wild, furious set of contortions that only the obscene
throbbing of the jig could catch. There was nothing
balletic here. When he was 'gone' or when it was 'over',
or whatever way you wish to describe his exit from the
field – from the theatre of war – exit, pursued by a . . .
bullet – only Shakespeare play I ever liked – I put the
poem in the pocket of my jacket. Too superstitious to let
it rest upon my heart. I survived the day.

I dried the paper over a candle that night and tried to
decipher what it was that he had written.

I was on his left as he fell

The boy with bright pink English face
A face and body designed for rugger scrums
And the village dance,
The fumbling of girls in a slightly drunken haze
And then marriage and children
And life lived almost in a trance.
That was his gentle destiny
For I knew him well
The boy on whose left I was as he fell.

I could make out a few more words of what I took to be the second verse:

I was on his right as he fell
A man much given to coarseness

I did not honour his silent request. Yet I felt no guilt. So many died that day and many-a-one may have had a poem, unfinished, lying near his heart. In my book – which brought me fame and a little money – called *The Short History of a Bullet* – I chose prose to trace a bullet's trajectory from the rifle of a German soldier, past the men it did not stop to the boy it felled – I used the fragment. The one critic who commented upon the verse – the others did not even mention it – found it the least convincing piece of writing in the book. I suppose I felt ashamed on his behalf. His talent was not as he had imagined, a fact he would have learned, had he been spared.

My second book, *Unfinished*, brought me further praise. And though it too was about the Great War, I avoided any reference to the poet on whose left I was as he fell.

I think that's enough. Thank you and goodbye.''

''A man of few words, as they say. I'm out of my depth with him. And only with him. I need to get my voice back, Max's voice, the one I've used for all this time. Where is it? . . . ladies and gentlemen – no. And now, ladies and . . . no, that's not it – AND NOW, LADIES AND GENTLEMEN . . . that's more like it, yes – that's it – my voice – I've got it back.

And now, ladies and gentlemen, we have a little chorus, a cacophony really. The panicky voices of those approaching death. We can hear them here. First softly, but getting stronger all the time. They're beginning to understand that after they pass through death's gateway they are approaching oblivion. They're trying to gather up something for the journey. Oh, come on, Voices. VOICES, WHERE ARE YOU? Remember, ladies and gentlemen, the young may die. But the old must. And they know it.

OK, Voices. And Voices, try not to trip over each other, don't fight for the words. You want to start with a little song and dance routine? Isn't that SWEET? Can't you hear the music and the dance steps . . . ?"

"He's been gone so long,
That it feels like yesterday."

"That's how we old feel. We remember best. Yes, it's true. We remember the things that count. Because we may have to look up old friends, you see. Wonder how we'll be welcomed. Can't say to John, who's waiting for me, I suppose, 'Did you know I slept with Annie? That time you were away on business. That long, long-ago old, sad, lovely, long fuck. Did you know that I licked . . .''

"Ssh, the nurse is coming."

"No, dear. No more tea for now, thank you. Memories interrupt tea time, dinner time. They interrupt my dreams of John, who I betrayed and of Annie, who I licked and licked. I think of them a lot now. Now that I'm near to what John knows already. The day and time it all ended."

"Nurse."

"Yes, Ellen."

"Write me a poem, Nurse. Go on dearie, for the children. To remember me by. Go on, it's nearly Christmas. Be kind, Nurse. Be kind, Nursey. It's a topsy-turvy world, when you know that soon the earth will no longer be beneath your feet. So please write me a poem, dearie, like Buffalo Bill."

"Buffalo Bill? Tell me about it, Ellen."

"I was married to an American once. Did I ever tell you that, Nurse? A Yankee. I married a Yankee. He taught me 'Buffalo Bill'.

Buffalo Bill's
defunct
      who used to
      ride a watersmooth-silver
                stallion
and break onetwothreefourfivepigeonsjustlikethat
                        Jesus
he was a handsome man
                and what i want to know is
how do you like your blueeyed boy
Mister Death?"

"Damn. Damn it. Ellen's fading. Hey, you out

there. Audience, did you get that last line? 'Mister Death' wasn't it? I like that line. It shows proper RESPECT.''

"Max, I hate these voices. They're not one of us, Max. And Ellen. We know Ellen's coming but not all of us are pleased. She's vulgar. And she sounds as though she wants to take over.''

"Listen, Imo, you all want to take over. Do you think I don't know that? Everyone wants to take over. No one is a bit player in his own life. Life is a fascinating monologue to the one who lives it. But not for the rest of us. God, you can be so pushy, Imogen. OK, OK, it's over to you now.''

"Thank you, Max. And be fair. It's my only speech, Max, and, it's bloody short.''

"Imo, listen to me. If you hit the right note with this you can walk away with the evening.''

"Not if I have anything to do with it.''

"Shut up, Tony. You've got your chance in a moment.''

"I thought I should sound more demented, Max.''

"No, Imo. She's not mad."

"Isn't she, Max?"

"Imo, let's say — just for a second — that she is mad. Madness is a great part for you. Remember all those great mad scenes? Ophelia, Medea, even dear old Hedda wasn't all there, darling. So go on. Let's have just a tinge, angel, just a soupçon of insanity. Stand here, under the cross. Just a touch of sacrilege, but He forgives all, they say . . . Though only God Himself could forgive this story. If He exists. GO ON IMO, TELL KATE'S STORY. QUICKLY."

"I walked through the village in my nightdress. And I smiled to think how fittingly I was dressed. An Ophelia, not in flowing silk, but cotton crisp, my hair loose but limp upon my shoulders. I walked so strongly. One step, two steps. I remember the journey well. I go over and over it, through the years, through the decades . . . Listen to me.

Onward I go. I am headed towards the canal. I have rejected the river. They all sleep now, it's four o'clock in the morning, no one is around. I want them to know I respected the beauty of the river. And also, I want them to know my last vision was not of the long-tendrilled willow trees. Such a thought might soothe them and that's not my intention. Perhaps I also feared temptation, a temptation which might have made me raise my arms towards the green, fragile, swaying ladder to catch at life. No. Damn them is what I say. Damnation, is what I call upon them, their damnation as well as mine. Let them know I chose the dirty water. Let *him* know, that they all know, I chose the dirty water. Let each one know I wore my nightgown, clean and cotton-white, stiff-starched for the filth. I am leaving my marriage-bed for ever. What a deceitful description of the piece of furniture, in which nightly, filth was poured into and upon me. And I close my nightgown round about me, my nightgown which has not protected me. No matter that I starched it rigid. His early angers at my armour have now become a vile excitement at its texture. I know, were I to switch to silk, he would find other ways to twist and turn me into a torn ribbon, ripped by him in his death-throe gurgles of delight.

He will know the meaning of the filthy nightgown, white beneath the muck. And they will guess. His friends who seem to like and respect him, and his mother, small and thin and wicked, who never warned me, when motherless, I married him. Wicked woman, she will know. I'm certain that she knows the awfulness I suffer.

She never speaks of her own husband and little to him when he is in her presence, which is very rarely. I know he is as vile as his son and that he throws his heavy viciousness on Emma Graceton. Emma Graceton, who I am certain does it for money. Her dresses are much more lavish than her husband can afford. She must do it for money.

There is the new moon which, they say, brings luck — and they also say is a sign of chastity. I laugh. Laughter is chuckling in me now, as I think about him looking at the nightgown, soiled. Not white. Not red. Just soiled with brownish blackness, the filthy slime of the canal, which I chose above the river.

I am now a wise woman, not a wise virgin. No virgin is ever wise. For virgins, like everyone else, think they need knowledge. Even if they do not long for this particular knowledge, they think upon their lack of longing. Unwise virgins. Roll your ribbon up tight. Keep it taut. After it has been ripped, there are painful shreds and then there is the final tearing, so that rent asunder, another may pass through the stretched and pain-stinging gap into the world. And sewn up again, is useless. The sheen has gone for ever and the ribbon rinsed in blood can be rinsed in water, but can never again be clean.

I'm nearly there. Slip slide in. Slip slide . . . And the

baby has not cried. She has been so good. Now I must place my hand over her tiny mouth and nose. And I laugh. I am cold and filthy and triumphant as I leave you, husband, sleeping your last quiet sleep in your empty bed. And listen to me now, hear me, husband, hear me in your sleep. You will never, ever be the kiss-king father of my baby."

"Don't you find that woman REPULSIVE? Do you know what her husband did, after they found her? But that's another story. Why don't you make it up? Go on, you can do it, of course you can. Everyone's a script-writer. Write the story of how she was forgotten. Did love destroy her, I hear you ask? No, darlings, sex was the killer. And whether you're flying towards it or from it, one slip and it's a free fall, angels, into death. And not 'la petite mort' of orgasm – we're talking the real thing here, darlings.

But did you know that eighty-one per cent of suicides are male? Does that surprise you? Vets do it most often, then pharmacists, dentists, farmers and doctors. Evidently, helping one's fellow man and looking after all those dumb animals just doesn't work, duckie.

Why did I choose this group? What an interesting question, madam! Why did I choose these people? Well, they were persistent. As in life, some people, like cats, just creep up on you. And remember, the people with the most interesting stories aren't necessarily the ones who talk. Oh, absolutely not.

I mean, over there is BRONSKI. He was tortured you know.

And JENNI who . . .

OH GOD, NOT YOU. I DON'T WANT YOU HERE. YOU ARE NOT WANTED HERE. YOU AND YOUR FUCKING SILENCE.''

"SHUSH MAX. SHUSH. Just listen. Listen to the silence.''

"I CAN'T BEAR IT. SHUT UP. SHUT UP.''

"Max, hush-a-bye, hush-a-bye. Listen, Max, I promise I'll talk to them for a minute. For you, Max, who hates the silence so. Listen to me, Max. I'm talking.

My daughter insisted I tell you this story. For years I resisted saying 'it's too sad, it's too sad'.

'But you're happy,' she'd say. 'You're happy.'

'Yes, I'm happy,' I'd reply. 'Is that unforgivable?'

'Yes.'

'I thought so.'

'Still, you're happy, Mother. So tell the story.'

'Is it so important that I'm happy?'

'Yes. It's more important than the story. I thought we agreed, Mother, that it's more important than the story . . .' "

"WELL GO ON."

"No, Max."

"YOU BITCH. YOU DO THIS EVERY TIME. YOU ALWAYS INTERRUPT WITH THIS ... BEGINNING. I'LL NEVER TRUST YOU AGAIN."

"Maybe it's all I'm meant to say, Max."

"JESUS. It's pathetic. Who do you think is interested in this fucking hymn of yours?"

"They might be, Max."

"Why? Give me a reason."

"Because I didn't tell the story. They'll remember the silence. Goodbye."

"YOU'RE NOT MY CHARACTER. YOU'RE CATH-ERINE SAMUELSON'S CHARACTER. And she can have you, darling, and she can have your creepy daughter, who never says much either.

Ah, they're gone. I think they've gone over to you, actually – the audience, always waiting to receive. The mother's just by your shoulder. Can't you hear the silence? Don't shiver.

LOOK, I WANT TO STATE THIS CLEARLY. I really am in charge. I could pick anyone to chat to you tonight. It's just a random collection of minds. But remember we're all part of the random sample. Ask one thousand people and they can tell you what millions think. So much for the INDIVIDUAL.

ARE THEY TRUE? WHO? THE ACTORS OR THE CHARACTERS? ARE THE CHARACTERS REAL? The answer's no, duckie. No. They are not. Realism, darling? What are you talking about? Looking for realism in the theatre? In the novel? In art? Detail? You want more detail? Like what did Oedipus have for breakfast? Why do you want to drown in the detail of what is not?

Now, I'll be honest with you. I mean, why not? What do I have to lose? Catherine Samuelson, remember her, so-called author, wanted another group. But I insisted on my choice. She sulked, you know, an artistic sulk. 'But I created you, Max,' she said. 'YOU'RE MINE.' 'Oh, grow up, Catherine. I'm here, duckie. I'm here for the duration. Let's negotiate.' But she's strong and I weakened. I suppose I felt embarrassed and a bit beholden to her. She accepted a compromise, a precis of voices. Can you bear it? Just a few more voices? No, they're not original stories. But then, neither is yours. I keep telling you and you just keep forgetting. Why?

'These characters are not real?' WHO SAID THAT? WHO SAID THAT? My God, aren't there enough real characters around you? In RE-AL life? No, you're right. There aren't. You need to believe in my little group here, don't you?

ISN'T THAT AMAZING! YOU WANT TO BELIEVE IN WHAT IS NOT, BECAUSE YOU CAN'T BELIEVE IN WHAT IS. YOU WANT TO BE MOVED BY THOSE WHO ARE NOT, BECAUSE YOU ARE UNMOVED BY THOSE WHO ARE.

And let me tell you, if you're not moved tonight, tough! These characters simply want to get across the fact that they existed. They'd like SOMEONE to remember them. OK? Is THAT TOO MUCH TO ASK? It's a hell of an effort for them, so don't be so fucking selfish. Anyway, why should a play move you? If you want to be moved just look around you. At those you care about in life. Do you care about anyone? Really care? Oh, apart from the family, darlings – that's ducking the issue. Why would you care about a character I made up, in the bath one morning? Ask yourselves, why? No answer? Let me give it to you, sweetie – because it's easier, that's why. There are no repercussions and the whole thing has a time limit. NOT A VERY IMPRESSIVE BUNCH, ARE YOU? YOU'RE JUST FUCKING LAZY, THAT'S WHAT YOU ARE. I'd better calm down. Just a minute while I take three deep breaths . . . um, that's better.

Right. Catherine Samuelson keeps wondering how many characters have been created since time began? Mathematically speaking. And where did they come from? And where the hell have they gone? Is there a graveyard for all those characters we've forgotten, in all those plays never performed, and all those words which no one reads. On and on she goes. In life, in art, same thing to her. But I wonder, is life just performance art?

Listen to this group, Catherine's little group. They're all talking about the end, as you might have guessed. Some endings come in what you could call the 'fullness of time' and are of course, everybody's favourite. Most people sincerely believe that's how their story will end. Then there are the surprise endings, which get all the attention. They're not fair because they happen to little boys and young mothers and men at the height of their powers. Those people become their deaths. First, listen to **Beatrice, the Brave**. Brava, Beatrice. Now's your time, girl. Off you go . . . ''

"He wasn't there when I was dying. He had other commitments. Family commitments. Another family. I drove him away. I had listened to his words so carefully I made him mute in my presence. My daughter said my sin was despair. Who am I to comment? I understood, I think. I'm sorry to burden you with the ending of a life you never knew. Perhaps you'll remember me."

"I'm sure they will, darling. Thank you. Now, **Simon. Simon**, you're on."

"Those who knew me then, always preface their comments with the manner of my death. Since they are my only chance of remembrance – I left neither children nor wife, being of a sexual nature which precluded the possibility of both – I must put aside my disappointment. They are living. They have the power. And the living are always ruthless with the dead. So I must rely on them.

I remember how frightened my thoughts were of oblivion. They seemed to leap from me during the crash. I could hear them, screaming down the road, in an ecstasy of terror crying, 'Hide us, hide us. Hide us in your mind. Give us space in your mind. We're dying too. It's not fair. The boy's gone, he's useless. Give us shelter. Give us shelter.' They seemed to find a resting place, for suddenly everything was quiet. And I knew I was dying. And that I'd better do it well, since now it was the only thing I'd ever do. My memory is filled with dreams of my future which I had to leave behind. Who will live my future now?"

"Simon was a diligent student, he loved his subject, philosophy. Poor Simon, who hears his mother over his grave in her silent, unbreakable rage. But when *she* goes . . . what can I say? Ah, well, on to **Tom**, actually, I like Tom a lot. He seems decent, you know. Listen to him. See if you agree . . .''

"While I lay dying, and my mother to whom I was all in all, finally understood that she was defeated, she cried out to me in desperation, 'Live in me, Tom. Live in me.' Her face, her mouth, came down on mine, open, as though to devour me. Her eyes were hot with life. She kept pleading, 'Come to me. Come.' And to soothe her, I whispered, 'Yes, mama. Yes, mama. I will. I will.' 'Come to me, Tom.' 'I'm coming, mama.' I didn't tell her what she seemed to have forgotten. That I would only live in her until she died. That even my life after life was terminal. It seemed too cruel to be truthful at such a moment and I never learned cruelty, dying so young. And so I ended as I suppose I began, with my mother crying out to me, 'Come to me, child.''

"Two boys. What can I say? I really like the way Tom tells his story. He's got dignity, that boy. Wasted, of course. **Evelyn's** next. I don't understand her. Pay attention, maybe you can tell me what she's talking about.''

"I never said goodbye. And he never said, 'Goodbye,

Evelyn.' We misunderstood each other in the last moments, as in the first. So I'm detached from those here who re-live their goodbyes endlessly, in agony. I think they're lucky.''

"Here's a man who for reasons I will never understand forgot his own name . . .''

"It was not my name. But when they called it I turned around, as though in acknowledgement and met a sudden ending. So sudden I hardly had the time to wonder who he was – this Colin Roache – to whose name I had fatally answered.''

"It's IMPOSSIBLE for me, that story . . . ah, here's little **Alice**. Only four. She's beginning to whimper. SHUSH. Be quiet. She's only a baby, really.''

"I was all rosy red on the carpet coughing rosy red onto the lovely blue carpet full of flowers and they looked so . . . surprised and mama screamed, 'She's coughing blood,' and I melted into the roses on the carpet and I went to sleep on the petals and I can't believe I ever was.''

"And now **John**, who doesn't want to say much. Doesn't want to upset the living. He's a nice chap. OK, John, as discreetly as you can."

"Later, when she called my name over lunch, I was in a state of decomposition. I died for a dream. And it wasn't even mine."

"When John was eventually found, a policeman said on TV, 'In all my years as a police officer I have never witnessed . . . etc., etc.' John held the attention of the audience for about a minute before the next news item – the break-up of a major pop group. There's fame for you. And now, on to the next. **Patrick** – who couldn't be stopped."

"I heard him calling to me. 'Patrick,' he cried, 'Patrick.' Each night as I lay in bed, I felt he was deep, deep beneath me. And I felt that some force-field pulled me to him. 'Join me, Patrick, I'm lonely. How can you stay there without me?' And so I left. I am fighting for the memory of life – as I remember it. I left the same way. I did the same thing. Well, I knew it worked. And as I fell asleep, I held his photograph to my face until our faces seemed to blend.''

"And lastly, here is **Penny**. So accommodating, so hopeless.''

"I remember life. I kept making adjustments. Then adjustments to the adjustments. Until I couldn't remember how it had originally started.''

"Well, that's the end of the 'Shorts', as I call them. And now at last . . . Aha . . . Aha . . . HERE HE COMES. HERE COMES TONY. Sauntering on. JUST LOOK AT HIM. Take him on trust, darling. Make an effort. He's got to believe in this character, Peter. Then he's got to convince you. And you, of course, must convince him of your belief in his belief. Could your life sustain this burden? He wants you to look at him being Peter, and think, 'Isn't Peter tall?' 'Isn't Peter handsome in his understated Armani suit?' Which, incidentally, took the biggest slice of the Wardrobe budget.

The thing about Peter – the character Tony plays – is, he's very, very pleased with himself.

He just loves himself. Peter won't tell you this, I
know, but he once sat on a train from London to
Edinburgh on his way to an important meeting
and kept telling himself, in rhythm with the
wheels: 'I am energy. I am energy. I am energy.'
Can you believe this man? Now, that is a very
important question, ladies and gentlemen. Who is
this man? Did I create him? Did Catherine
Samuelson create him? Or, are you thinking of
someone just like him? Could someone else tell
Peter's story? Or what he thinks is his story.''

''Max! I'm centre stage now.''

  ''Indeed you are. And you want your moment.
Well, here it is, duckie. CATCH IT. QUICKLY.''

**''Concentrate everyone. My name is Peter Bishop.
Have you got that?**
  When I, Peter Bishop, was twenty-two, an event
occurred in my life which caused me to leave England and
move to Paris. I had inherited a considerable sum of
money from my grandmother. With help from an adviser
– introduced to me by a cousin – I turned my inheritance
into a substantial fortune by the time I was thirty.
  My mother, whom I loved passionately, believed that
love was a virtue not just an emotion. Her second mistake

was to believe that virtue was rewarded. During her marriage to my father, she was slowly and emphatically robbed of this rather gentle and admirable belief. My father once told me that he feared my mother's imagination. 'She has lived,' he said, 'in a house totally constructed from her dream of me. Will I ever escape?' It is so difficult to escape the dreams others have of us. It's a form of murder.

I should perhaps, in fairness, introduce my father. When a man speaks of his father, he is always false. So, with an inevitable falseness — which I acknowledge — I will give you this short assessment of the man whose lust created me.

If you feel this description of paternity is crude, then you did not know my father. He believed that children should be protected from certain mythologies in life. For example, the mythology of natural parental affection. Thus, my brother Daniel and I were made aware that children are born into this world more often as a result of the desire for intercourse than from the desire for progeny. This de-mythologizing information was imparted to me at the age of eight, and to my brother, Daniel, when he was six. We were taught that the aspects of fatherhood which related to the protection, guidance and care of offspring were the duty attendant on the biological outcome of intercourse and not necessarily the result of natural affection.

Thus began for us a long series of separations of what my father regarded as 'The Truth' from 'The Mythology'. For example, the separation of the truth of the persona from the mythology of personality was undertaken in the arena of 'nomenclature'. The onomatopoeia of the word was emphasized in his violent pronunciation. Names, he believed, were fundamental to a disturbingly shallow assumption of individuality. His method of demonstrating our reliance on names led to much teenage anguish for my brother and me. 'Who are you? Are you just your name? Peter, define yourself and without recourse to titles, neither mine nor that of your mother, nor to any names.' Turning to my brother, Daniel – whom he'd then address as Peter – 'Do the same,' he'd order. My father's fierce sensibility to names remains with me still, as does an uneasy awareness of the dangers of the performed life.

In conversations with my father about our writing – both my brother and I were early cursed with the arrogant desire to communicate ideas – he would take us to task with the following litany:

'Who is the author?
    Who is the narrator?

Who is speaking?'

And, finally, 'Were you a witness?'

Fanatical about the study of the Greek tragedies, 'the encounter of man with more than man,' he constantly reminded us that the most terrible scenes in literature were revealed through reported action. 'And so it is in Life, boys' – though from the age of twelve he referred to us as gentlemen – 'little is witnessed, much is only overheard.'

'And now, gentlemen, since we have dealt with Life, to the matter of . . . The World . . .' His pauses, before and after, almost made one visualize the capital letters. The contrasting philosophies of the Epicurean, the Stoic and the Sceptic were sometimes discussed in relation to the conduct of 'A Life in The World'. However, an agnostic, he would more often ruefully quote the simple tenet of Saint Teresa of Avila: 'Be in the world but not of it,' to summarize his feelings.

Other tenets for Life – his own – were communicated to us as though from on high. 'Slay the deadening mythologies behind which so many hide, gentlemen; Silence the siren voices of religion; Beware of worldliness; Distrust the song of self.' My journey from childhood to adolescence was, as you can imagine, rigorous and demanding.

My adult life in Paris, however, was ordered and

extremely privileged. After the publication of two well-received books on the Symbolist period – a passion of mine – I felt it was not a wholly unnoticed life. I was grateful for that. By a certain age, some small point has to have been made. The opposite, total withdrawal, is of course equally acceptable.

I was married to Jacqueline. She loathed the abbreviated Jacqui. She was a small, clever, potentially vicious woman whose soul yielded early in its struggle against a venal nature. This nature had, incidentally, proved spectacularly successful. Her shop on the Rue des Beaux Arts, in which she sold a certain kind of fake jewellery, was extremely successful and, though everything lovely was beyond her means, she gleamed with a kind of deep, burnished, material wealth.

On certain occasions and in order to maintain the outline of a marriage which suited us both, I took her to her favourite restaurant – Closerie des Lilas – and then to an hotel room in a seedy part of Paris, where we had intercourse. This, I did not find unpleasant. Her fantasies were conventional and easily satisfied. The sexual motor of marriage should, I believed, be kept 'ticking over'. Otherwise the extreme of elective celibacy might lend a potentially dangerous, extra importance to the dalliances which we both acknowledged as an essential ingredient in our lives.

My own affairs had been numerous. Hers were fewer but of longer duration. My sexual nature was shallow and fed most happily on the surprise of a new body. I enjoyed the speedy learning of its lessons, followed by the respectful closing of the chapter. No one had fallen in love with me, nor I with them.

My wife's adventures had also been conducted with a certain discretion and, I would guess, the same attention to detail. Her partners in these liaisons were of a type. A reasonably successful actor; a journalist whose intellect had long lived on the edge of people and events which did not finally matter; the Chairman of a major television network, and the Director of a small bank. Sincere men, perfectly decent, average men, who appreciated my discreet wife, as, on each occasion I was betrayed, I appreciated theirs. Even, once, the wife of the Chairman during the fifth month of her pregnancy. Being childless myself I had long been fascinated by the copulatory problems encountered in pregnancy. I forget many of my liaisons, most in fact. However, I often think of the afternoon in May when penetration was achieved with infinitely less difficulty than I had imagined, though the position was one with which I was not familiar. It is my nature that, should a man consider cuckolding me to be without consequence, he should continue with that illusion only at my pleasure. Making it clear to a man who has slept with your wife, that you have enjoyed the same privilege with his, is a delicate matter and one which I carried off with great panache.

I was aware of my own high intelligence. Over the years, I gave much thought to the layers of life which required investigation in order to create an existence which was bearable. There was, at its most obvious, the physical reality of oneself. And the necessity to maintain in a reasonable state of efficiency the machinery on which one was so dependent. To this end I swam daily and three times per week I attended judo classes. I had therefore the physical confidence of a man who knew he could effectively defend himself. Against whom would I wish to defend myself? Against anyone who at any time threatened me, even momentarily. My physical ruthlessness was disciplined by my martial arts training. My worldly success was based on my psychological power to intimidate and, at will, to repel. When described as a bully, I always replied with a polite, 'Thank you.' I had great respect for the tenets of Machiavelli, a writer who I believed was much maligned.

Realization of one's sexual nature was, I believed,

vital to the total well-being of both male and female. Mine, as I have stated, was basically shallow. Just as a young, beautiful woman in pursuit of riches or a place in society can twist her sexual nature towards acts of which she would not earlier have dreamed, with a man for whom nature had not designed her, so, also, can a man be driven to a certain level of sexual experimentation – especially in the pursuit of one who is loved by another. These intricacies were part of human nature. They neither surprised nor depressed me.

As to my psychology and, indeed, my philosophy of life, well, Gide's statement, 'One is alone, the self is entirely unknowable' and the contradictory Greek 'Know thyself' juxtaposed themselves constantly in my mind. Forgive the implied arrogance, however, in truth, I was always an arrogant man. A number of years of Jungian analysis convinced me, that in my case, the effort to 'know myself', was not actually of any serious import to anyone, least of all myself. With relief, I fell into the more relaxing, slightly amoral belief that I was unknowable. However, I felt an intelligent effort had been made and, indeed, took some pride in my endeavours.

Spiritually, I was attracted to Rome and its thrilling absolutes. The abdication of the search for Truth inherent in its required belief in Mysteries was wholly delightful to me. That aside, it was in my opinion the most aesthetically pleasing religion, combining certain classical, intellectual precepts with a controlled romanticism. Perhaps it is that unusual combination which is the genius of the Church of Rome. I attended instruction on a regular basis, reached a certain level, then admitted with resigned relief that an act of faith was beyond me.

So, I lived 'the examined life', and found it to be an interesting experience. I was content to have kept despair at bay for over twenty-five years. I considered this to be no small achievement. I was physically in an acceptable condition for the life I led. I was sexually fulfilled within the limits of my nature and my past. I was attuned to the psychology that played its acknowledged, though slightly hidden part, in many of my actions, dreams, thoughts and feelings. Spiritually, I had delved as deeply as I wished to go. I had ticked each element on the human shopping list and I had made myself as close to a man as others seemed to be.

This existence of mine was passed for the most part in a house of some nobility in Paris. I have noted with interest that the others spoke little of their environment. I can only assume they lived more in their minds . . . or souls, than I did. So, I will attempt to describe this environment with, I hope, the kind of telling brush strokes which will also imply my feelings about my domain – my set.

My apartment in Rue de Rennes in the sixth arrondissement was large. A grand salon ran the entire length of the house. Six floor-to-ceiling windows led out onto a tiny terrace, with a view of les Jardins du Luxembourg. This room was entirely decorated in cardinal red, and decorated with antiquities rather than paintings

My library, the decoration of which was a surprise gift from my wife – I had been away for three months – was an exact reproduction of a nineteenth-century English library. The original panelling was transported by her from England: a charming and thoughtful gift.

Perhaps a more detailed physical description of my wife, Jacqueline, might hold a certain interest for you. She was small with a disciplined, voluptuously-formed body. A bust that was slightly disproportionate to her waist was perhaps the essence of her erotic appeal. She had excellent legs and light-blonde hair which was feathered – I believe that is the word – to frame her pale, rather petulant face.

It was from this woman and this apartment that I set out on the twelfth of October and returned to England, for my annual visit to my father at Grantley Manor which

I would, in time, inherit. I am always accompanied on these visits by a young woman of a certain physical type, tall, pale and with red hair. My father and I both know the reason for this but we never discuss it. We have discussed little for years. There is little to discuss. He knows me well and is not much interested in what he knows. That's all. He is not much interested in me. Bitterness was such an inadequate response and over time I found it best to withdraw, which he had barely noticed . . ."

"MAX? MAX, IT'S ME."

"WHAT ARE YOU DOING HERE? WHAT THE HELL DO YOU THINK YOU'RE DOING? WE'RE IN THE MIDDLE OF PETER'S MONOLOGUE. GET OFF. GET OFF, FOR CHRIST'S SAKE."

"Max, I'm lonely."

"Well, tough. Now get off this stage immediately. I DON'T WANT YOU TO DO THIS EVER AGAIN. UNDERSTAND?"

"But I'm lonely. And I just want to be heard. I want to be heard, please. In anything, I'll be happy in anything."

"Happy? Are you crazy? Just get off this stage NOW."

"But Max, I have a tale to tell. I want to talk about her. My dead wife. You just won't let me. And I'm the one who remembers her best. And you won't let her talk either."

"You're interrupting things here. So for the last time, GET OFF THIS STAGE. OK?"

"Please, please, Max. I really mean it this time. I really am sincere."

"Really? You astound me. You're sincere about it all?"

"Yes, I mean I thought sincerity was essential."

"Do you mean complete sincerity?"
"Yes."

"Quite extraordinary! I honestly don't know what to say to you. Well, I mean, of course, I know what to say but you understand so little, you almost make me weep."

"Why?"

"Because of the consequences, for you"

"Max, I'm not certain I'm up to this. But I want to try. Really, Max, I want to try."

"Oh, come on in then. I suppose we have lots of room. And lots of rooms. The Room of Extreme Goodness, rarely full. The Room of Last Knowledge, bitter place, I can tell you. The Room of Dark Ecstasy, there's always a queue for that one, but people never visit it twice. The price is too high. The Room of Casual Evil. The door's always held ajar to that one. People lean against it and just fall in. Which one is for you? Let me think. Sit over there. I'll come back to you. Maybe I'll come back to you.

I'M SO SORRY, PETER. THIS IS A DISGRACEFUL THING TO HAPPEN. AWFUL FOR YOU, PETER. AND YOU WERE DOING SO WELL. Still, I suppose, it's just like life. Do you remember, Peter? Interruptions, interruptions. Nothing finished. Nothing resolved. Just snippets and then more interruptions. Until even interruptions ceased. Ah, Peter, you've been joined by the beauteous, OH, JUST LOOK AT HER, LADIES AND GENTLEMEN

. . . just look at her . . . our Lovely Lady of Lust. She has the look of women who are looked at, doesn't she? Don't be embarrassed, sir. We all feel it. Well, perhaps not, but you know what I mean. She's going to play some games. But I'll tell you now, she's a bit out of her depth. She may have been Head Girl, and God knows, she's often given head. Very smart girl, always giving head, and not just the way you think, you bad man, but she's out of her depth here. She almost makes you drown with lust, doesn't she, sir? They always hate that idea, don't they? Women hate to think we're drowning in our lust for them. They don't know what it's like, do they, sir? Isn't it amazing how those who arouse it so rarely feel it!

Anyway, Peter, back to your little scene with Lady Lust — which you remember so well. He's word perfect, actually, folks. Just listen to him. Peter, are you ready? You remember that last dinner with your father Theo?''

''Yes, I remember, Max. I remember her voice . . . And his. His was the last voice I heard. It seemed to echo. It still echoes – I hear the girl now and her stupid questions . . . .

'Do you believe in the luck of houses, Mr Bishop?'

'What do you mean, young woman? And you may call me Theo.'

'Well, that some houses are unlucky, Theo.'

'I believe certain houses find unhappiness a welcome guest. But I don't believe in luck. I'm not superstitious. We ran a large house, as you can see. But it didn't fit anyone.'

'Believing in luck or ill-luck is hardly superstitious.'

'How would you describe it, Peter?'

'Simply as an assessment of reality. There are benign and malevolent forces at work in the world and good luck and bad luck is arbitrary.'

'Surely we make our own luck?'

'Young woman, I find that such an arrogant state-ment. Don't you, Peter?'

'No, Father, not arrogant exactly. But wrong. Definitely wrong.'

'Would you say this was a lucky house, Peter?'

'No, I wouldn't say that, Father.'

'Why isn't it lucky?'

'She's obsessed with this idea of luck, isn't she, Peter? Please, madam, don't bother to give me your name. I'm too old to have an interest in anyone new. At my age, you know, one's met everyone. The entire cast, so to speak. And one knows it's just another interpretation. However, I suppose I must answer your question. Manners, courtesy to the ladies – and so few of them are worthy – means I must answer you. Perhaps it was not a lucky house, young woman, because good people were destroyed here and you can, I think, feel their . . .'

'Despair, Father?'

'No, no, ours is the despair, Peter. You know that.'

'The Jesuit from whom I used to take instruction described it as the unforgivable sin, Father.'

'Did he indeed? Why on earth did you take instruction? After all I taught you? God, what a waste of time! Silence the siren voices of religion. Do you remember nothing? Anyway I couldn't bear my sins to be forgiven. I think I would go mad. They, my sins, are me. In fact I cannot think of anything about me which is different from anyone else, except my sins. They are entirely my own.'

'Oh, I helped, Father. Don't you remember? I made some small contribution.'

'Indeed you did, Peter. And you were very young at the time. You astounded me with your capacity. These are unpleasant memories. Let's talk about Our Lady of

Lust. I have no appetite for her other than to feast my eyes. Her voice I find singularly flat and unappealing. Do you agree, Peter?'

'Her voice is not her greatest asset, Father.'

'Would you like to stay here with me, Lady Lust? I offer intelligent depravity and superior perversion. Will you say yes, young woman?'

'But you don't like my voice.'

'We've already discussed your voice. Try not to be boring. Maybe I'll let you stay for this year, maybe for next. It's a Picasso-like obsession, a different woman every few years. Yet, after all those women, they say the last word on his lips was the name of Apollinaire, whose masterpiece was a work of pornography. We're terribly foolish about sex, don't you think? Forgive the way I talk. But you may have so little time.'

'*I* may have so little time, Theo?'

'Isn't it wonderful how the young always assume they will outlive the old? There's no guarantee you know. I have on a number of occasions buried men young enough to be my son.'

'And of course, Father, you buried your son.'

'Yes. Yes. Oh, that was a very long time ago. A very long time ago. Did Peter ever tell you what we did?'

'No.'

'Peter rarely tells anyone. He's very secretive. And no one talks to me so I have no trouble keeping secrets.'

'Tell them, Peter.'

'No, Father. You tell them.'

'Shall I make it a short story?'

'Short? Yes, I think so, Father.'

'You're right. Their lives were very short, so it's more fitting. He loved a girl who died. He loved a girl who died. He loved a girl who died. I need the repetition of it. These words break the silence for me. The line means nothing to anyone else. I repeat it in order to emphasize what it meant to me. He loved a girl who died. And he did not believe it was true and joined her. I like to think she smelled of virtue. Is that short enough? I failed. I failed to tell him death was real. Or he simply didn't believe it. Young people often don't. Indeed, a lot of people don't.'

'What did he do?'

'Ah, the voyeurism of it. Why do you want to know? Oh, well, why not? A week after she was buried he went to her grave and dug down to her coffin, opened it, swallowed his mother's sleeping pills and was found dead the next morning. How many lines was that? Let me count. Six? Eight? And to tell such a story? I never forgave his mother, never forgave her, for the pills.'

'Nor me, Father, for sleeping through his leaving the house. In the week after her death he had slept in my room. He had seemed so frightened.'

'I forgave no one, Peter. I forgive no one. His face was almost glued to hers with . . . Oh, you must know the effect of sleeping pills. This was not a fairy tale. Which is why I will not pay lip service to the mythology of grief. The romance of death has enough practitioners. Are you angry, young woman? Ah look, she is full of feeling. I hope it's anger. Angry women were best, as I recall. My appetite, for that was all I had left afterwards, was for angry women. Cruel when young, older I grew worse. Don't look bored, young woman! I am old. I'm entitled to my reminiscences. Also, I have things to explain to Peter, maybe for the last time.'

'Oh, Father, you're in excellent health . . . ?'

'Peter, dear, I fear you misunderstand me. Again. Now, where was I? Oh yes, when I was younger there was one woman. There is always only one woman. Did I ever tell you, Peter, that I liked to dress her in fur and then later in leather. Masculine and feminine. And I gloved her in silk and in cotton, white cotton. And into her ears I poured vague obscenities and whispered a mantra of putrefaction so seductive in its oily balm that she swung her filthy hair – aah – into my mouth and I ate her. She had red-haired pubes, a connoisseur's delight. Is this vile? Does this disturb you, Peter? My poor Peter, I do hope so. And you, young woman? As I thought, women rarely object. Men object on their behalf, I find.

'Did you know I was powerful, once? Oh yes, I made waves as I came to shore. When I walked into rooms, others followed. People were always anxious to meet me. But in the end you cannot rule a world you have destroyed. They flee me now. But I had only one vice. People, like nations, have a tendency to one particular vice.

You, Peter, are a weak man. Unlike me, you do not have the strength for vice. But do I care? You see, Peter, for me, you have a certain degree of irrelevance. I suppose you know that I always preferred your brother. But he's dead. Now, ask yourself, what father would not celebrate his last remaining son, who, by the act of penetration of a fertile female, should be capable of reproducing me – in one form or another? Why do children rarely think of that? But I do not lust for any child of yours, dear boy. If it can only be carried forward by you I would prefer my name to become extinct. Fortunately, your wife, that French woman, has given you no children. Perhaps extinction becomes you.

'Of course, since, unlike you, I know my fertility, I

could take this young woman and by dint of diligent fornication impregnate her myself. What an interesting thought! My failing powers could perhaps, by mouth or tongue, or by various positions she might be inveigled upon to undertake, still produce one last burst of fluid and thus give me an heir worthy of my name. Have I gone far enough to destroy you? And yet I have not moved from my chair. A little ode to the power of words, whether true or false, you will never know. But you will remember them. Or perhaps we only remember the things that should have happened.

'She, the one who left me when she saw the abyss from which I could not climb, she might have saved me. But by then even my poor wife had had enough of me. Sometimes I used to feel, oh, a twinge of something, for having wrought such destruction. Could it have been guilt? I can't remember. I admired my wife, I think. I outlived her. Of course, I had to listen to the tributes but then it was all over. Oh, believe me, I disdained my cruelties. However, I couldn't quite desist from them. They became a habit. You see, in a sense, I feel they were a sign of energy. At least a spirit, even if malevolent, moved in me. My passion for — The Woman — had such force. It was impossible to walk away from its compulsive madness. I never expected the doom she carried with her but, my God, how I raced towards it. And my wife had been so generous, nauseatingly understanding. She almost lusted for cruelty and, wearily, I supplied it. "You two are killing me," she'd say, over and over. "You two are killing me." Sometimes I wanted to laugh. It's strange how often the catalyst for evil is good. It seemed grotesque that she could feel so much when I felt nothing for her. I told her things I hoped she would remember and most of them were lies. "Comfort yourself; you would not seek me if you had not found me," I shouted to her once and I let her think the line was mine. When one ceases to love, one is rarely kind. I knew a man once who, by the time he realized he hated his wife, found out she was dying. It seemed unfair, monstrous even, to tell the truth. After all, she was being magnificent. It was irrelevant of course, her courage, but in a way it was moving.

'My wife had a kind of courage. But I tested it to breaking point. Once, my wife found me in the garden, I was consumed, consuming my lady. For six days I had fed her soft, white cheese and celery and figs and plums and dark chocolate and ice-cold wine in the evening. We looked at her until she ran away. We just stared at her. I am, you see, rotten, I'm rotten. I was not always like this. I didn't start out like this. Once, I wished to be otherwise. But a fatal ennui overtook me. I ceased to live years ago and it's now too late. Perhaps each life has only one lesson to teach us. I had a long life. And I deserved it. It's been a just punishment . . . Do you feel life's a punishment, Peter? I hope so. Oh, I do hope so . . .' "

"WHAT DOES IT ALL MEAN? WHAT DOES ALL THIS MEAN? WHO SAID THAT? WHO INTERRUPTED . . . ? WHO ASKED THAT QUESTION? STAND UP, PLEASE. YOU WANT THE CONNECTION? 'Only connect,' as the man said. My God, after all I've done for you, all you want is the connection. What's the connection? The dead in search of a life? Characters searching for remembrance, trying to defeat oblivion? Christ! Four characters? Six characters? Oh darlings, use your fingers.

I gave you their lives. And their lives after death. And now you want me to tell you WHAT IT ALL MEANS. I think you're looking for a fucking plot! Are you children? What's the plot of your life then? Does it have a plot? Well, you arrogant bastard, who's writing it then, eh? Answer me that. Who's writing the plot of your life?

AND THE OTHER TWO, DARLINGS? WHAT TWO? THOSE SILENT WOMEN? BUT THEY'RE ON YOUR

SIDE OF THE FENCE NOW. THEY'RE NOT WITH US ANY MORE, 'NOT ONE OF US'. LISTEN TO THEM. IF THEY EVER SPEAK, LISTEN TO THEM. THEY'RE ETERNAL. PERPETUAL MOTHER, PERPETUAL DAUGHTER. LISTEN TO THE TWO WHO KNOW THE WHOLE FUCKING STORY, BUT WON'T FUCKING TELL IT. EVER. They're beside you now. Can't you hear them whisper? That old ode about silence.

I'm tired. I'm tired of you all.

CAST, COME OVER HERE, I JUST WANT TO SAY YOU'VE BEEN ABSOLUTELY WONDERFUL. WELL DONE. BRAVO. BRAVO. But the audience! You've probably wasted your time with them. They're a useless bunch. That's an aside! Oh grow up you lot, don't be so touchy.

'Christ, I must have a drink.' I HEARD THAT, SIR. I HEARD THAT. It's time for your drink, is it? Just got to have a drink, have you? Oh, all right, get your drinks – all of you. Shall we see you later? Perhaps not. All too morbid for you, darling? Still, don't forget while you're out there drinking, we're waiting for you to come back. We're always waiting . . . for you.

WHAT'S THAT YOU WHISPERED? I'm not real

enough? Would you believe in me more, if I told you I lived in a red room on Gloucester Avenue, and my fridge was filled with turkey rashers . . . ? DON'T GO. NOT YET. OH, ALL RIGHT BUT COME BACK FOR THE SECOND HALF. DO. AND TELL YOUR FRIENDS. I'll be here tomorrow night. And the night after. I'll be saying exactly the same words. Will your dialogue be any different tomorrow, or the day after? For the next six weeks, I will be like the philosopher Kant, by whom men could set their watches as he started his walk each day at exactly the same moment. At eight o'clock each evening I will speak the same words and if I die I have an understudy, with whom I am familiar, in a manner of speaking. Are you familiar with your understudy? Have you studied him, her? Remember, he's, she's studying you.

YOU'RE THINKING OF GOING? Leaving the theatre? What's your hurry? It's the same destination to the last moment. AND, AT THE LAST MOMENT OF SELF, IS THERE A LAST MOMENT OF SUPREME UNDERSTANDING? I don't think so, darling, I don't think so. And will they catch the real you?

'. . . After you've gone,
there'll be some crying.
After you've gone,
there'll be some sighing . . . .'

Too young to remember the song, darling?

Oh, all right. Go back to whatever little story was on your mind. They'll all stop one day, just in the middle of something, with everything half-finished. But if you've got time – it is a real question, I'm not just being polite – if you've got time, go back to whatever you were doing before I started. GO ON. GO BACK TO WHAT YOU'VE FORGOTTEN SO EASILY, SO QUICKLY. STOP GAWPING AT THE TABLEAU. IT'S BEEN DONE BEFORE. IT'S NOT THAT DRAMATIC, DARLINGS. GOD, I CAN'T RELY ON ANY OF YOU TO REMEMBER. YOU ALWAYS FORGET, ALWAYS. ANY NEW STORY AND YOU'RE AWAY. HAS IT OCCURRED TO YOU, THAT'S HOW YOU'LL BE FORGOTTEN? OH, IT WILL TAKE SOME TIME. THOUGH NOT AS MUCH AS YOU THINK. OH NO, NOT BY A LONG CHALK. NEW STORIES WILL CROWD OUT YOURS. YES, BELIEVE ME. EVEN FOR YOUR NEAREST AND DEAREST. OH, PISS OFF THEN. BACK TO YOUR STORY, SUCH AS IT IS . . . . FOR AS LONG AS IT LASTS . . . BACK TO THOSE YOU'VE FORGOTTEN, AS YOU WILL BE FORGOTTEN. I HATE YOU ALL.''

NINE

A week later. An hotel in the country.
  "Good afternoon, Mr Bolton. It's room 142."
"Thank you."

What am I doing here? How can I do this? God, how can I do this? The last time you were with us, Laura, I couldn't really see Sarah's body, only yours, Laura. It's not for pleasure. It's to know myself again, even for seconds. You have no needs now, Laura. You have nothing now, Laura. You have nothing.

And I have everything. I am here in my body and I have memories of you, with me. Now I have my time with Sarah. Sarah who loves me. Sarah who has me now. How can I let this happen? I was always lazy. I am still lazy. I am a lazy man and now I'm also tired, which adds to the laziness. I need firm ground. Please understand, Laura, I need firm ground. For a time the firmest ground for me was when I stood beside your grave. And once upon it. It was the only certainty I had, once.

"Sarah, darling. Come in."

"Andrew, I'm so sorry I'm late."

"And I'm sorry it's still so often in hotels."

"I do understand. Don't worry. It'll be better in time."

"You shouldn't be so patient with me, Sarah."

"I don't know what love is, if it's not patience."

"But, Sarah, you say that about everything I ask of you. Which is far too much. You say 'I don't know what love is if it isn't kindness.' 'I don't know what love is if it isn't understanding.' Maybe, Sarah, it's just pity?"

"What's wrong with pity? There's some love in all pity. And some pity in all love."

And I remember the lines you loved, Laura – 'A pity beyond all telling, Is hid in the heart of love.'

"How do you know? You're so young, Sarah."

"Everyone knows these things."

"Everyone doesn't."

"You're wrong. It's just that everyone doesn't act on them. Anyway, experience doesn't necessarily teach you anything. Sometimes quite the opposite."

"Sarah, Sarah."

And you went away, Laura, for twenty minutes. No.

I lie to you, Laura, as I lie down now with Sarah. You went away for an hour. Which is a long time under the circumstances.

TEN

My mother-in-law, Jane, was involved in an accident. She swerved to avoid a group of people who stepped off the pavement in Trafalgar Square, and crashed into a stationary truck. Amazingly, I still can't get over the coincidence, but Sarah was in the group. It was an accident, a terrible, unforeseeable accident. I am determined on this reading of events. And I will not countenance any other. Jane was quite badly injured but she survived. Sarah called the ambulance. She's such a competent girl, she never panics. I love that about her. Sarah went with Jane to the hospital. For a time I feared they'd become friends. What could I tell Sarah? Fate, of a kind, bringing them together and all that. Isn't that terrible, Laura? I feared they'd become friends. Well, they didn't. Sarah said, despite her best endeavours, that your mother resisted. I'm grateful to your mother for that, Laura.

I visited her, of course. I had not been in a hospital since . . .

Jane lay in the bed, part of her body hidden in the purity of fresh plaster and her head by bandages which obscured her forehead and her hair. I remember thinking – death will be discouraged by this armour. And when I smelled the air I thought – no smell of death here.

"Jane. Jane?"

"Ah, Andrew. How kind of you to come. What a drama! Perhaps your Miss Samuelson could write a play about it." Jane's voice almost chimed out, resonant, defiant, unbroken. Its power shocked me. An unnerving contrast to her wounded body.

Is she going to . . . ? To what? Confess? To what?

"Middle-aged mother visited by dead daughter's husband – and looking for – is that Catherine Samuelson's kind of subject, do you think?"

Nothing. She's going to say nothing. But what is there to say? It was an accident.

"Your Sarah's a nice girl."

"Yes. Yes, she is."

"A bit like Laura, I thought."

"Oh, I don't think so. I don't see a resemblance." How can she say that? What is she trying to do to me?

"No? I do. If only resemblance or semblance was

enough. How easy to go on with the semblance of the other. The drugs have dulled the pain but I find my mind quite strangely clear. It jumps, you know, from here to there — from you to her, to her. Which her? Sometimes I have to ask myself — which her? Don't go, Andrew. Stay. Talk to me. Play any good?"

"Yes. Yes. I thought so."

"Jack read a review to me — evidently it's a series of monologues spoken by the dead. How strange. A bit close to the bone, as they say. Did she choose you, Andrew, do you think, as the perfect interviewer?"

"Choose me? Good God, no. It was just timing, a special kind of timing, I suppose. You read about it every day — actress — just separated — brings special depth to part of rejected wife. Gay novelist illuminates story of young man dying of AIDS. In any audience there's always someone watching their own story, at least in part."

"I met her once."

"Who?"

"Catherine Samuelson."

"You met Catherine Samuelson? But when?"

"Oh, years and years ago. Perhaps 'met her' is a little too grand. She came to lecture when I was at Cambridge. I was one of the two girls who looked after her, you know, took her to the lecture hall and showed her where the lavatory was, and so on. As I said, nothing grand.''

"What was the subject?''

"Oh, I remember that all right. Her paper was 'The Necessity of Pain'. I thought her horrible – really quite horrible. She told a story I've never forgotten about an aunt of hers who had lost her husband and daughter in the war. In one of the camps – I can't remember which – which in itself I suppose is awful.''

"It was a long time ago.''

"Does that make it any better, Andrew? Time? Does it make it any better?''

"I hope so, Jane. I do hope so. How did her story end? About the aunt?''

"Ah yes, the aunt. Do you know what ECT is?''

"Electric shock therapy?''

"Yes. Well, the aunt was fine for a few years evidently and then quite suddenly she simply gave up any interest in living. Nothing seemed to affect her. All pleas were useless. Her husband – her new husband,'' Jane smiled at me, a kind of swollen smile, "there is usually a new husband or wife . . .''

I said nothing. I wanted to hear the story.

"ECT was popular at the time and it was suggested she should have it. She seemed not to care either way so they went ahead. She made a full recovery and lived happily . . . she's dead now, I suppose.''

"So . . . what's the story?''

"Ah yes. Well, ECT kills short-term memory, you see. So it killed certain memories of her first husband and child. I remember Catherine Samuelson explaining that it was like a second murder . . . a second death for them. She didn't seem to care about the aunt very much. Saw her only as the repository of their lives.''

"Perhaps you're being a bit harsh on her, Jane. It's debatable at least.''

"Maybe, but she had a fanaticism I didn't like. I remember now something she said which I'd forgotten for years — 'our past is memory and our future oblivion. We are forever balanced between the two.' Play anything like that?''

"A bit. Yes.''

"I'm finely balanced at the moment, Andrew. I'm not certain which way I shall fall. I kept a diary for a while. I've stopped now. Can't write with this arm, or move much because of the leg . . .'' She motioned to the leg in plaster. "Do you know the Plath poem about being in plaster?''

"No.''

"Ah, it's good. It's very funny. Here . . .'' She

motioned to the table. "I like the first verse. I think it's page 116. Will you read it to me? Oh, come on, Andrew, don't look like that. I'm the one who's uncomfortable."

What could I do? She had trapped me. I picked up the book and began to read.

"In Plaster
I shall never get out of this! There are two of me now:
This new absolutely white person and the old yellow
   one,
And the white person is certainly the superior one.
She doesn't need food, she is one of the real saints.
At the beginning I hated her, she had no personality –
She lay in bed with me like a dead body
And I was scared, because she was shaped just the
   way I was".

"She could be a very witty poet, you know . . . Jack's good on poetry. It brought us together in a way. Though even in that we were different. I loved the romantic poets, Wordsworth, Tennyson. But he was trapped with his Greeks. Occasionally a little Milton, Eliot – though I learned to love Eliot. I suppose in those days my mind was more like an exuberant English garden and his was, and still is, formal, organized like those classical French gardens. Ah well, at least it was something between us. And he's been good about all this. In his way, which is not my way. But there are things you don't know when you marry. Yet they're quite important – different ways of grieving . . . but then who marries with grief on their minds? Poor Andrew. You can go now. I'm tired. And so are you. I'll be here for some time. Perhaps you'll visit again?''

". . . Yes, of course I will . . .''

I kissed her, trapped in her bed, in her plaster, a thought which soothed me, and left the hospital.

I had a date with Sarah. I was taking her to see *Les Enfants du Paradis*, a film which I first saw with Laura. Is this unforgivable? Perhaps. And as I hurried towards Sarah, waiting for me in the foyer, I thought of the main female character, Garance, and wondered as I gazed at Sarah why *femmes fatales* were rarely English.

ELEVEN

George Bonnington spoke to me – as I knew he must. It was before lunch, the kind of Sunday lunch I once attended with Laura at her parents' house. 'Plus ça change, plus c'est la même show'. But what play am I in? Could Catherine Samuelson tell me?

"You and Sarah seem to be getting very much closer."

"Yes."

"It's serious then?"

Why do people say that? 'Is it serious?' as though it were a fatal disease.

"I care about her a great deal. She's been wonderful, simply wonderful."

"Yes. She's a wonderful girl. She's our only child. We've always been aware of the dangers of being over protective."

Only child. Just like Laura. Why hadn't I been struck by the coincidence – significance – before?

"Do you feel you need to protect her from me?"

"Good heavens, no! No. We like you enormously, Andrew. But I wonder have you considered the difficulties for you both – setting out together with such a . . . sadness . . . in your recent past? I wanted to talk before things went any further. I reconstruct the body after trauma – but it's never the same body, Andrew, however well I do my work."

"I know I'll never be as I was . . ."

"Good. But do you know who you are now?"

He sounded a bit like Max. Only he didn't mock. What can I say? I am a widower – one of many. I think I know the lines now. And I – like many a widower before me – am 'with', in all the various meanings of the word, another woman, his daughter. But I didn't say that. It's not my style.

"I think so. And I will think more about what you said before . . . ."

"Please understand, Andrew, we – Grace and I – are not in any way opposed to your relationship with Sarah. As I said, we like and admire you a great deal. Let me assure you, I'd speak frankly if I didn't. I don't believe in interference but I do believe in truth. Sarah may have told you we strongly disapproved of her relationship with Claud Masters and when he decided to stay with his wife, we were extremely relieved.''

"*Claud?* Claud Masters?"

"Sarah's never told you this? Oh God, I'm sorry. This is terrible."

"No. No, she hasn't told me. But I'm sure she'll tell me in her own good time." There was a long, embarrassed silence.

"Did Claud get Sarah her job?"

"Yes. Yes, I think so . . . That's where you met, wasn't it?"

"Yes." I was really shocked. I just didn't know. Claud brought us together. How extraordinary. And the Catherine Samuelson interview? He's the MD. They don't normally interfere in programming. Still . . . a word here . . . well, does it matter? Does it honestly matter? What difference does it make after all? When you've lost everything, as I have, perhaps you're less greedy. Perhaps the death of those we love smashes the ego. Our powerlessness has been proved. Maybe her affair with Claud, this history that she now has, will make me love her more. Yes, that's right. Though she's young, she too is 'going on' after a certain kind of loss. Yes. It really could make me love her more. So, in a sense, Claud

Masters brought all this about. And does it matter? Does it honestly matter?

After all, in so much of the story of our lives, can we ever know who is the author? Who is the narrator? Who is speaking?

TWELVE

The Catherine Samuelson interview was much praised. My producers are going to enter it for an award. They say I caught her. But they are wrong. Though I tried to handle it tactfully, she refused to answer any questions about her long relationship with Arthur Byfleet, other than to say "it was a sin for which others paid a higher price than I did."

The deliberate confusion about the interval which was, of course, the end of the play, was explained thus: "I have found that much in life which is considered interval is, in fact, finality."

She seemed strangely full of doubts about what she had done with her life, quite unlike her confident performance at our lunch. She spoke passionately about the dangers of what she described as "the seduction of what is not". And wondered whether her time might not have been better spent in the exposition of what she saw as the "harsh and holy comfort of what is".

She then said something about literature which provoked an enraged response from a well-known contemporary of hers. "I begin to wonder," she said, "whether literature is not in fact as much an opiate as religion. Lives examined and explained, matters resolved or particular meaning found in the lack of resolution. The reality is: we witness little; people drift in and out of our lives; much is only overheard; and setting our lands in order is no more than a valiant act of defiance." I thought, is this despair? The unforgivable sin?

Later in the interview she astonished everyone by dismissing her play *The Living Truth* as "political diatribe". Evidently one small theatre company had particular difficulty in persuading her that their desire to stage a revival was wise. But when I watched the interview later, what I had originally considered humility sounded more like arrogance.

Scenes from *The Mourning Site* and *The Gate*, looked quite good but the plays were clearly not going to last. My producer and I decided against showing the tableau at the end of *The Book* – when Theo murdered his son, Peter, leaving Lady Lust, a now un-beautiful puppet-like creature, mute with shock – though to be fair, it worked well in the theatre.

Instead we transmitted Max's opening speech straight to camera. I felt it came across well and most critics seemed to agree. I asked her if there was the possibility of an alter creator, as well as an alter ego and was Max, perhaps, her alter creator? "We kill the voices of the dead so often," she said, "that perhaps accidentally we also kill characters waiting to be born. Maybe Max had a hard time coming into the world and therefore rejected his 'mother'." This, with a note of bitterness.

Which led me to explore why she had not had children. She replied, almost casually, that she had in fact had a child out of wedlock (she actually used this phrase) a girl, who had died as an infant. She denied that the 'Letter to a Dead Child' which she had shown me at our lunch, had been written by her. "The child in that letter was much older," she snapped.

When I tentatively broached the subject of her comment concerning the Holocaust, "In this the Jews behaved like Christians", she replied, "I lacked reverence and I was consumed by anger. However, I still believe that there is a kernel of truth there. Let us move on. I don't wish to discuss this issue in the context of my work. I am not a genius nor am I morally profound. Both of these qualities, or at least one, is required for such an understanding. That is why, though I wished to write about the dead, I created characters whom art dignified. I will not use lost lives to dignify my art.'' As she spoke, I wondered, is this true?

Later, when I watched during editing, her face as it faded from the screen disturbed me. It looked as though it held a secret she refused to confront. And I thought that certain deaths cannot be overcome. It is as simple and as terrible as that.

THIRTEEN

Francis Byfleet's book came out too late for me to read it before the interview but I suppose the publisher would say the timing was good, coinciding as it did with the run of the play.

Driving home alone from Sarah's flat – how long can I keep leaving like this? – I heard part of a late-night radio interview with him.

"Yours is hardly an unbiased view, Mr Byfleet."

"Of the woman, no – of the work, yes."

"Are you so certain of your professional integrity?"

"Absolutely. I'm a certain kind of chap." Laughter – from Francis Byfleet.

"How do you rate her?"

"Inelegant question, if I may say so. Sorry, I should be charming you, I suppose. Otherwise you'll nail me to the wall, eh? Don't worry, just teasing. In my book I stated that when I analysed each of the plays I came to the conclusion that Catherine Samuelson is capable of great insight into one, sometimes two characters in each play. The others, however, are often there to illustrate her reading of the main character. 'Character is action' is not part of her philosophy and the plays lack a certain dramatic tension which even in these post-Beckett days is, I believe, essential.''

There then followed an unbelievably pompous analysis of *The Living Truth*, which it turned out was one of the interviewer's favourite plays and the antagonism between them became even more pronounced. I suppose therefore in a sense it was a 'good interview'.

''Can we turn to your decision to tell of your father's long affair with Catherine Samuelson?''

''Oh, come now, you're not suggesting I should have ignored it?''

''No, but you seem to make it the central issue in the book.''

''Please remember it was the central issue in my mother's life. It led her into despair and, eventually, alcoholism.''

''Is Catherine Samuelson responsible for all this?''

"Yes."

There was a silence. The interviewer waited. Well done.

"An unfashionable view, I agree. Let's just look at it like this. Catherine Samuelson is admired as a woman of high moral integrity. Yet for over fifteen years she ruthlessly conducted an affair with my father while all the time refusing to let him leave his family. Her version of morality."

"It seems quite admirable to me."

"Does it, young woman? Have you ever been sexually in love?"

"What?"

"Have you ever been sexually in love?"

"Mr Byfleet, this is becoming impossible."

"Well, just let me finish. My mother was passionately in love with my father. She suffered the almost unbearable pain of sexual rejection. My father and Catherine Samuelson believed that keeping the family together while they conducted their grand affair was a triumph of virtue. In fact, of course, marriage to my father would not have suited Miss Samuelson in the least. She is, or sees herself as, a free spirit. Her life is a brilliant construction. Her *art* and a great passion (I don't deny it was a great passion) were allowed to complement each other within a structure morally acceptable to *her*. Let me tell you, young woman, Catherine Samuelson's entire life is an amoral edifice of twisted values. The victims, my mother, my brother and myself . . .''

''Your brother is Ben Byfleet, the poet.''

''Yes.''

''But you have both established successful lives and careers.''

''My mother is dead. Her life was cut short by the pain Catherine Samuelson caused her.''

''And your father? You don't seem . . .''

''When a man speaks of his father, he is always false.''

''That, Mr Byfleet, is a line from Catherine Samuelson's new play.''

''Well done. Indeed, it is. It's also a line often spoken by my father in my presence. Catherine Samuelson stole it. In fact, there is one monologue in the play – the Theo Bishop monologue – which I consider an act of theft. Many of those lines were first spoken by my father.''

''What are you saying? That the character of Theo Bishop is based on your father?''

''Not on my father as he was before Miss Samuelson. I . . .''

"And the son, Peter Bishop? Could he possibly be based on you?"

"No, and again no."

"Mr Byfleet, I'm afraid we must finish there. Thank you for joining us this evening and that's all from us tonight. Next week I will be talking to Astrid Aaranson about her new novel *Frozen*. Till then, good night and read well."

The Book was a moderate success. Though the scene at the end between Peter and Theo Bishop — will I ever now just see them as characters? — came in for one savage attack, 'Pure melodrama, bordering on pornography.' But I remembered Catherine quoting Yeats: 'Do you think it horrible that lust and rage Should dance attendance on my old age.' None of the critics seemed to find the fact, that most of the characters were dead, difficult.

I had a little card from her some time ago saying her next piece would be a two-hander, like a 'singles game of tennis'.

Did the play affect me? Who can tell? I knew she had written the part of Widower before she met me. There are many of us, I suppose. And the character of Annabelle, in certain moments, reminded me of Laura. But as Catherine Samuelson said: little in life is resolved;

much is only overheard; much, in the end, is only an echo. Perhaps she's right, we are constructed for forgetfulness — the forgetfulness that we will be forgotten.

However, it's something she said at our lunch which comes back to me most often. "Happiness is a decision. Make it. And don't cry."

FOURTEEN

Some form of separation is taking place. Some part of me is falling away. I am slipping guiltily, even furtively, into another life. And in another life I could cry out, "Haunt me. Haunt me, Laura," as teenagers we once called out, "Haunt me, Cathy," to add intensity to it all. But I am not Heathcliff . . . nor was meant to be. Am an attendant . . . widower. One who waits, pathetically, for some rhythm, to bring him back to some form of life. One who will make his bargains, a woman, some sweetness, a little life for a little man.

Well, is there anything wrong with that, Laura? Is there anything wrong with that? What do you want me to do? Answer me. Answer me, Laura. Do you want me to die, Laura? Is that what you want? You want me to die? For Christ's sake, say something, Laura. Say something. I'm so angry.

Another date's come round. No one knows except us?
US? Except me. Does your dead body remember, Laura?
Does it know? No one knows how you look on this date
now. Not you. Nor I, who once knew every line of you.
Now, there is not knowing and not wanting to know.
What went first? Was it the breasts I bit? Or was it your
legs, on which I used to play a not-so-innocent snakes and
ladders? I can't speak of your eyes. Who can speak of
eyes? Why not? We know they too must go. Where are
your eyes, your lovely eyes? Who has them? What has
them? Don't answer, Laura. Perhaps it's still too
early . . . The rest, too obvious to discuss in its
disintegration, in the disintegration of you, Laura, darling
Laura. Can you hear me as I listen now to others? To
Sarah . . . to Sarah now. Oh, Laura, Laura, can you hear
me listening to Sarah?

Over time, as I listened, Sarah-Sarah made the speeches
you would expect her to make. They were full of feeling,
and they were sincere. They had within them half-
guessed-at feelings, half-understood, from her childhood
witness of adult scenes. Lines from some long-forgotten
film she had seen, a thought from the romantic novels of
her adolescence, an idea from *Jane Eyre*, not *Wuthering
Heights*. Lines, perhaps from her affair, to which we

never, in fact, refer. Maybe she sees me as a Mr Rochester, who is not blind, or as a decent Max de Winter; and you, Laura, as a kind of benign Rebecca.

I liked the way Sarah-Sarah said her lines. Weary with the battle against such a determined love I surrendered to her rescue attempt, and I was grateful to do so. There were certain, unspoken conditions, of course. I knew that you, Laura, would now be pushed along by me on your journey towards oblivion. I will no longer say in public, "My wife, Laura", now I will say, "Have you met my wife, Sarah," "Sarah, come over here and meet . . ."

Friends will not talk so readily of you, Laura, and not in front of Sarah. It's a gentle form of assassination. All the sins in this are those of omission, in order to protect the living from the vanquished. As time goes on, knowing for certain that there is no retribution from the dead, a certain carelessness with the facts takes hold. To be honest, darling Laura, you would already barely recognize yourself, that old self, were you to listen to us now.

And so, Sarah-Sarah will gradually devour the public role you had. And to those private flesh to flesh moments you will, in time, be a less frequent visitor. We have our own rhythm now, Sarah and I. It's not all that different, it never really is. Small tendernesses that reveal the almost old-fashioned sweetness with which she bound me to her, certain sounds or movements, nothing momentous. Eros touched me lightly, I believe, and perhaps I was not built for the extreme. Though I wonder about it, of course.

After much anguish, I decided to invite my ex parents-in-law to my wedding. They declined; and I regretted the invitation. I had been misunderstood. I was ashamed, and as always in these cases, I was then a little angry at my own shame, and angry at those who caused it. The barrier rose further and you, Laura, could no longer plead their case. I am, in a sense, free to deal with them now as I please, in a way I could not before. And to be honest, Laura, I enjoy the company of George and Grace more. Jane was always . . . difficult. Even in my mind I go no further than this. And your father's philandering becomes more and more distasteful. They say he's going to leave your mother this time. Laura, how can I say this to you? I never liked him. Sorry, sorry, Laura. Grace and George, whom I admire, are easier with me. It's a more relaxed, playful relationship. Are you hurt, Laura? I can't help it. I'm going on, Laura, and you're not. That's all really. It's an idiotic image but I sometimes think we met on a train and you got off at an unscheduled stop and I went on. Just that. I went on. Then I moved to a different carriage, I met other passengers. I don't know when my stop will arrive. But I do know that until then, I will go on with Sarah. It's called courage, resignation, responsibility. It's a betrayal as well.

Anyway, Laura, Laura, whose name I always loved, what do you have to say to me, Laura? What do you say, Laura?

My doctor tells me I am suffering from a form of depression. Still. Even after Sarah. I left him. Just like that. Which was something I would never have done before. He talked to me about some grieving process. I'm in section three and I said, "Fuck you." Even my sadness is labelled. Nothing's a discovery any more. I know I was labelled, widower, lost his wife, first wife, any wife would do. Honestly, Laura, wife is what you were, and I seemed to have lost you. But I've found a new wife, Laura. I've found a new wife. That seems to be all.

I am not depressed. I am simply a rational man who is sad because his wife, his first wife, died. I intend to remain a little sad about that for ever. I can see that the love I had was not so overwhelming, that it could not in any of its facets be replaced by another. I eat with, I sleep with, make love to, go on holidays with another. I am a lazy, shallow man, who did the expected thing and I got over you. I went on with my life. And why not? Who cares? Fewer and fewer about you, Laura, and why should they? You have to ask yourself that, Laura. Why should they?

Sarah is pregnant. I am very pleased. "Yes," I say, "I really am very pleased." "Yes. Grace and George are thrilled at the thought of a grandchild. Yes. It's a first for them. Yes. It's a first for us all."

And it's true. It's a first for me. I, Andrew — your Andrew — will have a child, Laura. A child whose laughter you will never hear. A child to whom you will be a shadow, a shade. My shade. My lovely, lost shade. A new life is about to begin. And it's mostly thought of as a blessing. But it's sad for you, Laura. You could say, Laura, it's another nail in your coffin. And you know what, Laura, I'm inclined to agree.

I have a son, Laura. My son's name is John . . .